HAYCORN SMITH
AND THE
CASTLE GHOST

JOHN KACHUBA

Cover design copyright © 2023 by Niki Lenhart
nikilen designs.com

Published by Paper Angel Press
paperangelpress.com

ISBN 978-1-959804-67-3 (Trade Paperback)

10 9 8 7 6 5 4 3 2 1

FIRST EDITION

for
Evelyn and Wolfgang

ACKNOWLEDGEMENTS

My thanks to my beta readers and editors, Chris Tebbetts, Sara Bennett Wealer, Debbie Combs, Nancy Henry, Kathy Lorenz, my grandson Ethan Patterson, and my wife Mary. Special thanks to my grandchildren Evelyn and Wolfgang Yosmali for their insights into what kids are reading these days and why, and my granddaughter, Riley Driver, whose inability at the age of three to pronounce *acorn*, gave rise to our hero's unusual name.

1

SOMETHING SPLASHED IN THE RIVER.

I carefully parted the weeds, peering into the darkness. My hands shook.

"It sure is dark out there," I whispered to Budge, who hunkered down behind the rock.

Something splashed again.

"I heard *that*," Budge said, rising to one knee. "What do you see? Is it the Frog?"

The Loveland Frog. Budge and I had spent almost every night the last two weeks at the Little Miami River looking for the creature. It had been maybe ten years since two Loveland cops saw the giant beast one night by the river and shot at it. Plenty of people believed it was still out there somewhere. People like us.

Whatever it was, it was moving up the river. Splashing. Coming closer.

"Hand me the light! Quick!"

Budge thrust the flashlight at me. I grabbed it, turned it on, and aimed it across the water. Mist floated over the river like ghosts.

Budge peeked over the rock. "I don't see anything," he said, "except … *that!*" He jerked the light in my hand sharply to the left.

"What the …? Jeezul-Pete!"

Two red eyes glared at us through the mist.

"It's the Frog!"

Budge was ready to bolt. I caught him by the arm. "Shut up! Don't move! Maybe it hasn't seen us."

Suddenly, I had the urge to pee.

We froze. We were so afraid, it never dawned on us to turn off the light. We stood there like idiots, the red eyes coming closer. We heard the thing panting. Hideous.

"Goodbye, Haycorn," Budge whispered.

The creature was so close we could make out a large black shape below those freaky eyes.

Then it barked.

We looked at each other.

"Woof?" Budge said, just as Mrs. Riley's Doberman trotted up out of the river, shaking water off, soaking us.

"Stupid dog!" I said, "Go home!"

We watched it run off into the night.

"Guess we're done here?" Budge asked.

I sighed. "Looks like it. You know, we may *never* catch the Frog."

He patted my shoulder. "Maybe next time. But I've got to get going anyway. Merv will kill me if I'm out too late."

We trudged up the riverbank to the street where we had left our bikes. *Yeah, maybe next time.*

•   •   •

My name is Haycorn Smith.

I know. Go ahead. Laugh. You wouldn't be the first. But laugh all you want; Dad says my name is an old one and famous. Some duke or something in England, a long time ago. That's cool.

Still, there's always some jerk dissing me about my name, and sometimes I just fight back.

Which really ticks off Mom. She's on our town's city council and is *in the public eye*, as she likes to say, but Jeezul, what's a guy to do? Wasn't she ever twelve?

Dad was twelve once. He tells me not to get into fights but then he says he knows they can't always be avoided, which to me sounds like, *sic 'em, Haycorn!* The bad news is that I'm not really all that tough. The good news is, we're all getting older and there aren't that many fights anymore. We all just talk smack. It's cooler and doesn't draw blood.

And when it comes to talking smack, Budge Shifflet's the champ. He's been my best friend ever since he moved up here from Virginia. His mother always calls him "Budge" and that's how we all know him. Funny, though, I'm not sure what his real name is. Walter, I think. Budge's dad is short and stocky, like a fire hydrant, not at all like Budge, who is tall and spaghetti thin. He doesn't talk much, but he can put you down in three words; "pencil-necked geek" is Budge at his best. I think he learned how to talk like that to survive, since he's the only boy in a family of four girls, three of them older than him. Any time I feel bad about being an only child I spend a few hours at Budge's house. I feel a whole lot better after that.

Budge and I hang out a lot at the Little Miami River, which winds right through the center of Loveland. Sometimes, we ride our bikes on the trail that runs along the river. When we can scrape up some money, we'll rent a canoe from Bruce's, under the railroad bridge, and paddle down the river. It's a pretty river, with big white sycamores lining the banks. The Shawnee Indians called them "ghost trees." The river's not very deep, except in the spring when it runs high with rain and snow. Sometimes, the river floods Nisbet Park and downtown Loveland. One time, Mom and I put on waders and inspected the damage after a flood. The water had risen right to the top of the park's amphitheater. Looked like a giant swimming pool.

Mostly though, we hang by the river, sometimes fishing, but pretty much just talking and watching the water go by. I like to watch the great blue herons on their stilt legs fishing in the shallows.

On some nights, we might hunt for the Loveland Frog.

This is no ordinary frog, by the way. Those cops, years ago? One was on patrol when he saw something in the water. In the dark, he couldn't tell what it was. A man? An animal? He got out of his car and started down the bank, his flashlight lighting the way through the rocks and weeds. The thing didn't move. The cop still couldn't tell what it was, but it must have scared the bejeezus out of him, because he called for backup. When another cop rushed to the scene, they stepped cautiously on the rocks along the bank, drawing closer to the thing in the water. Suddenly, this beast leaps at them out of the darkness. It looks like a huge frog with glowing red eyes. The cops scream like little girls, yank out their guns and start blasting away. They miss. Whatever it was disappears in the night, never to be seen again. This is a true story, I swear. It was in the newspapers.

We were kids when that happened. Older now, we waste quite a few evenings looking for the Frog. We aren't the only ones, either. One of Mom and Dad's friends sometimes stays out all night with all kinds of electronic gear.

Loveland is a quiet town. Big houses—some of them McMansions—nice lawns, little crime. But then there's the Loveland Frog. How do you explain that?

"How do you explain that?" I asked Mom one night. She had just returned from a city council meeting. She was still wearing her dress clothes but had plunked herself down on the couch with an iced tea. She looked exhausted.

"How do I explain what?" She held the cold glass to her forehead, as though she had a headache.

"The Loveland Frog."

She sighed. "Are you still on that kick?"

"I was just on the Internet again, reading about it."

"Sometimes I wish the Internet had never been born."

"It wasn't born," I said, "Mister Google invented it."

She gave me a sour look. "Mister Google?" She kicked off her shoes and curled her legs on the couch. "Okay, fine. What do you want to know?"

"The cops saw it like ten years ago, right?" She nodded. "So, what's happened since then? Has anyone else seen it?"

Just then, Dad entered the room. He stood in the doorway, blinking at us from behind his glasses. They made him look nerdy, but I knew he wasn't a nerd. Dad was pretty cool, actually. "Hey, it's time for *Survivor*," he said. "Anyone want to watch it with me? They're in Costa Rica now."

"I'd love to go to Costa Rica." Mom pulled back her chestnut-colored hair, readjusting her ponytail. She took a big gulp of her tea. "How come you never take me to Costa Rica?" she asked Dad.

"Bugs, Sweetheart. Big ones. Big creepy crawlies." Dad wiggled his eyebrows like crazy caterpillars.

"Mom?"

"In a minute, Hay. Wait a second, Ron," she said to Dad, "you think I'm afraid of bugs?"

"Uh, yeah."

She set her iced tea on the table beside the couch. "Where did you ever get that idea?"

"Mom? The Frog?" I said.

She didn't pay me any attention. Instead, she zeroed in on Dad with her Snake-Eye expression. Dad was in for it. I've learned to get out of her way when I see that look. Dad was a slow learner.

"Where?" He turned on the TV. "Have you forgotten the Everglades? That little camping trip before we had Buddy, here?"

"You mean the camping trip where we *made* him," she said.

"Hell-o, I'm still in the room," I said. "I can hear you."

Dad held the remote in his hand, but he was looking at Mom. It wasn't *Survivor* on the screen; it was *SpongeBob SquarePants*; a better choice, I thought. "Whatever, Anne. All I know is, *someone* was afraid of the bugs."

"If you mean the clouds of mosquitoes that were everywhere, finding their way onto any part of exposed skin, into any nook and cranny and I do mean *any...*"

Jeezul! TMI. On TV, a starfish wearing a pirate's hat chased SpongeBob. I skulked off to my bedroom. Mom and Dad never even knew I was gone.

Look, I love my parents, I really do. They're great. Sometimes, though, they're clueless. They can be really embarrassing. And gross. I can't get far enough away when they're like that.

I flopped on my bed with a Harry Potter book—one I'd probably already read a million times—and let it take me away from the noise in the living room. Magic. Books always do that for me. I lose myself in them in no time. The Potter books are cool, but I'm also reading a lot about ghosts and ghost hunting, and that's way cool. That stuff really happens, unlike the Harry Potter stuff. It's right there in black and white and on TV, too.

Harry was flying around in a mean game of Quidditch when my cell phone beeped. A text message.

HEY, HAY

Only Budge thinks that's funny, and he says it all the time. I mean, *all* the time.

HEY, I wrote.

SUP?

NADT. U?

BORED.

ME 2.

I won't bother you with the details; nobody wants to read our text messages. Budge wanted to know if we could hang out at the castle after school the next day, which sounded cool, so I told him yeah, sure.

AWESO, he wrote, C U.

I went back to Harry Potter, but couldn't concentrate. I kept thinking about the Loveland Castle, as it was called, although its real name was Chateau Laroche. It had been a long time since Budge and I were last there. On weekends you could go inside the castle. That's when the Knights of the Golden Trail, the guys that ran the place, were there to let you in and give you a tour. They all called themselves *Sir* this, or *Sir* that. I think they really believed they were real knights, even though one was a barber and another stocked shelves at Kroger. Whatever, the place was still incredible. Inside, there were flags and banners and suits of armor. Swords and axes hung on the walls. It was all pretty sweet.

I knew the castle wouldn't be open after school, but that was okay. I decided we'd go anyway.

Math was my last class of the day. I hate math, and my grades prove it. I flunked math in sixth grade and had to have a tutor over the summer. Yeah, that was fun. Like having a tooth yanked. The tutor was this geeky guy with really thick glasses and an accent. He always said my name like "Hi-corn." I had to call him Mister Kashir. His breath smelled like tuna fish.

Somehow, I squeaked through seventh-grade math but now I still had to get through my last year at Loveland Middle School. Math is boring, boring, boring. If it wasn't for the fact that Ama Yendi sat only a few seats from me, I would not be able to stay awake. She was smart, much smarter than me. And pretty.

Math scared the bejeezus out of me. I once had a dream where all the sixes and eights and nines were snakes twisting around my feet trying to pull me down. They were going to square-root me.

After school, Budge and I rode our bikes to the Loveland Castle. The road down to the castle was steep, narrow, and twisty. You took your life in your hands trying to ride it, so we walked the bikes down to the riverbank and left them under a tree. It was cloudy and the river looked like it was made of steel. There was nobody at the castle. No surprise.

I get goose bumps every time I see the place. I don't know why, except that it's way cool. Awesome. Exactly like a real castle. It's built with stones dragged up from the river and it has arches and towers and all that castle stuff. Mom says that one man built it all by himself. It took him years to build. She says he was an old man when he died and that he still hadn't finished it. That's why the other guys are there now, the Knights. They're finishing the job he started.

"Look!" Budge pointed to the square tower at the front of the castle. "Check it out."

A big black bird squatted on top of the tower. A vulture. We picked up some rocks and chucked them at the bird, but he was too high up. We moved closer. Before we could get him, he spread his wings and flew off over the river.

"Take that!" Budge said.

"We missed him, dummy."

Budge shrugged. "We scared him, though."

I approached the solid, wooden castle door, studded with about a million iron nails. "Think we can get inside?"

"I don't think we should," Budge said, looking around nervously.

I tried the latch anyway. "Nope. Locked," I said.

We wandered in and out of the stables that never held any horses, and through the terraced garden alongside the castle, where a steep hill rose behind it. If I were an enemy trying to capture the castle, I'd just get up on top of that hill and roll boulders or something down on it. Maybe, boiling oil. I'd read somewhere they used to do that in the olden days. Must have hurt.

Once, when I was at the castle, there were some guys dressed like knights, with armor and stuff, and they were whacking each other with these fake swords. They were hitting each other really hard. The swords banged off their big soup can helmets and sometimes a guy would get knocked down. Nobody ever got killed, though.

Now, it was just me and Budge, and we didn't have swords.

"It's kind of creepy here, don't you think?" Budge said, as we walked through a series of stone arches.

"What do you mean?"

"Well, it's so quiet and all," Budge said.

"Could be because there's no one else here, Einstein?"

"I know. That's not what I meant," he said, still looking around as though expecting someone. "Do you think anyone died here?"

"What? You mean like knights?"

"I don't know, anyone," Budge said.

"Probably not. Wait, what was that?" We stopped in a passageway between rows of stone arches. It was dark in there. "Did you hear that?"

"That scratching noise?" Budge said, looking around.

I nodded. We stood there and then we heard it again. It sounded like someone scratching a nail or a stick on the rock walls. "There … that." My palms were sweating even though the air was cool in the passageway. I felt a lump in my throat.

"Oh, crap!" Budge's eyes went wide as Frisbees.

Something moved in the shadows near our feet. Budge yelled, or maybe it was me, I don't remember, and we ran out of there into the daylight. We stopped outside the castle, a safe distance away. We were breathing hard. Neither of us could speak.

I saw movement along the ground beneath the first arch. A small, dark shape humping along. A groundhog.

"Hey, Budge," I said, pointing to the animal.

It sat up on its hind legs as if saying "goodbye" to us.

Budge laughed. "If I was a knight, I would have whacked that weasel with my sword."

"Yeah, right. And it's a groundhog, not a weasel."

It wasn't that we were still afraid, really, but it was getting late. We had to get home for dinner, so we grabbed our bikes. Budge walked ahead of me. As we started to walk the bikes up the road to where it was level enough for us to finally ride them, I could have sworn I heard a laugh from the darkness behind me.

2

"WHERE HAVE YOU BEEN?" Mom said, as I walked into the kitchen. She was sliding a frozen pizza into the oven.

"At the castle."

"You know I don't like you going there alone, Hay."

"I wasn't alone. Budge was with me."

She sighed and wiped her hands on a towel. "That's like being alone," she said under her breath.

Mom doesn't like Budge all that much. Well, it's not really that she doesn't like him. She thinks he's a little slow. Lazy, too. I guess maybe he is, but Budge is a good friend. He'll do pretty much anything I want to do. You can't have a better friend than that.

"That place can be dangerous." She started taking dishes out of the cupboard. "It's right on the river and it's an isolated location. What if one of you fell into the river? What would you do?"

"I'd stand up and walk out." She squinted her eyes at me. "It's pretty shallow, Mom."

"You know what I mean."

I shrugged as I rotated back and forth on the chair at the counter. "Okay." She took three glasses down from the shelf and placed them on the counter. "Mom, tell me again who built the castle. I forgot."

"A man named Harry Andrews. Everyone called him Sir Harry."

"Did you know him?"

"Not well. I saw him a few times at the castle. He was always working on it, right up until the day he died. He was in his nineties, I think. Here, go put these on the table." She handed me the plates and glasses.

"How did he die?" I asked when I came back into the kitchen.

"Oh, it was a terrible accident. He was working with hot pitch on the roof of the castle when he somehow caught his pants on fire. Poor man. He died in the hospital a few days later."

"Wow! That's awful."

"Yes, it was horrible. Everyone loved him. He was famous and not just here in Ohio." She opened the oven and looked inside. "Go call your father. Pizza's nearly ready."

Dad came in from the garage where he was tinkering around with something and washed his hands at the kitchen sink. We had no sooner sat down at the table than we heard music coming from Mom's pocket.

Rah-rah-ah-ah-ah-ah!
Roma-roma-mamaa!
Ga-ga-ooh-la-la!
Want your bad romance.

Lady Gaga. Or as I called her, Lady Blah-Blah.

Mom took out her phone. "Hello?"

Dad and I munched pizza while she spoke on the phone. Between calls about city council stuff and her job at the county health department, Mom's phone was always going off, which meant that I had to hear Lady Blah-Blah over and over again. Sometimes I think Mom put that ringtone in there just to bug me.

"In the pool?" Mom rolled her eyes. "Wonderful. Okay, yes, tomorrow." She returned the phone to the pocket of her jeans.

She did not look happy. Dad gave her a questioning look.

"We had to close one of the pools in Cincinnati. They found feces in it," she said.

Feces. I loved that word. "Some kid crapped in the pool?"

Mom frowned. "Yes, Hay, but we say *defecated*."

"Do we have to say either while we're eating?" Dad's pizza hung suspended halfway toward his mouth.

"Sorry. Anyway, I have to go over there tomorrow to check it out," Mom said.

"That's gross. Why would a kid do that?" I asked.

"Give it a rest, Hay," said Dad.

"It wouldn't be the first time," Mom said, "and kids urinate in the pool all the time."

"For Pete's sake, Anne, do we have to hear all this right now?" Dad said.

"Sorry."

"They *pee* in the pool, too?" I said.

"Haycorn! That's it. Knock it off."

I shut up then, seeing Dad was getting peed himself. I couldn't help wondering what those kids were thinking. We ate our pizza in silence. I looked at Dad. He didn't seem angry anymore but there was a strange look on his face. Sad, maybe worried.

"I got a call from Tom today," he said, finally.

Mom set her glass down on the table. "Oh, no, Ron!"

"Well, it's only a rumor. We don't know anything for sure yet."

Mom didn't say anything. She just sat there looking at him. I knew something was up, but didn't know what, so I kept my mouth shut.

"All we know is that a unit out of Dayton is being deployed," Dad said.

So, it had something to do with the Reserves. Dad's in the Army Reserves, has been for a long time. I didn't like the sound of this. Neither did Mom.

"Iraq?" she said.

"Afghanistan."

"Oh, dear God!" Her voice was so small I almost couldn't hear her.

"That may be all they need."

"But if it's not?" Mom said.

Dad shrugged, but didn't say anything.

As you can guess, none of us were very hungry after that. Mom and Dad went outside to the back deck. I figured I should probably leave them alone. I went to my room.

It wasn't as though we didn't all know Dad could get called up at any time. It seemed like a lot of Reserve guys were going. I knew some kids at school whose fathers were already over there. I just thought because Dad was so old, thirty-something, they wouldn't take him. I mean wouldn't they think he might have a heart attack or something at that age? But I knew if his unit got called up, he'd have to go with them. I just hoped they were all old guys, so nobody would have to go. Anyway, Dad said it was only a rumor. There had been plenty of rumors before. Most of the time, nothing ever happened.

I lay on my bed and sent a text message to Budge, telling him that Dad might be called up.

SUKY, he responded a few seconds later.

Y.

GRAMPS WAS IN NAM, Budge wrote. HE SAID IT WAS SHIT.

I thought of that Cincinnati swimming pool. If they could close the pool overnight, maybe they could close the war just as easily.

We were off from school the next day because of a teacher in-service day. I had no idea what the teachers did that day and really didn't care. All I knew was that we had a day off. Budge and I rode down to one of our favorite fishing spots by the castle. Mike Kreutzer and Sean Baer went with us. Mike is cool, but I could live without Sean. If he hadn't tagged along with Mike, there's no way he would have been with me and Budge.

We dropped our bikes and walked along the river. Budge kept nervously glancing over at the castle.

"Are you alright?" I stopped with him and let the other two go on ahead.

"Yeah, sure. I'm just watching out is all."

"For what?"

"I don't know. Anything," he said.

He gets that way sometimes. Weird. Like he's seeing something invisible to the rest of us, or hearing things that we can't hear. He stops whatever he's doing and sort of stares off into space. Maybe he's tuning into aliens or something, I don't know. Maybe, like Mom said, he's just slow. Whatever it is, it creeps me out.

I remembered the last time we had been at the castle and the laughter I thought I heard behind us as we left.

"Do you see something, Budge?"

"No, not really."

"Not really? Either you do or you don't." He was making me nervous.

He shook his head. "No, nothing."

I looked at him for a moment, trying to read the expression on his face, but there was nothing. "Alrightee, then, let's do some fishing."

He snapped out of it and we caught up with Mike and Sean, who were already dangling poles into the green water of the Little Miami. The four of us spread out along the rocky shore, the castle looming on the hillside behind us. I dropped my line in a little pool where the water swirled and let it drift. Budge was about a dozen feet or so upriver from me.

You're supposed to be quiet when you fish. Three of us were. Sean wasn't. He kept talking and talking, running his mouth about God knows what. I tried not to pay attention. Then he started bragging about his father, who was also a city council member. Mom didn't have a lot of good things to say about Mr. Baer. I had been dragged to a few city council meetings and had heard him talk. He talked big for a short guy, and he was so full of himself. Now Sean was going on and on about all the great things his father was doing for Loveland.

I really didn't want to hear it. "Hey, Sean, we're trying to fish here. Be quiet."

He shut up, but a few minutes later, he was back at it. Yeah, his dad was going to bring a sports complex to Loveland, a convention center, even a velodrome.

"A what?" Mike asked.

"A velodrome. You know, for indoor bike races," Sean said.

"Like in the Olympics?" asked Budge. Sean nodded. "Wicked!"

"Come on," I said. "In Loveland? Are you kidding?"

"That's what my dad said. A velodrome."

"And where's he going to put it? In your back yard?"

"Funny, Smith."

"That's a load of crap," I said.

Sean put down his fishing rod and turned to me. "Listen, if my dad says he's going to do something, he's going to do it."

"Forget it, Sean," Mike said.

"No, I won't. Are you calling my dad a liar?" Sean took a step closer to me.

Budge came up behind me and I handed him my pole. "You said it, Sean, not me."

Suddenly, he shoved me. I slipped on the wet rocks but didn't fall. I heard Mike yell *Sean!* I guess trying to call him back, like a dog that had gotten loose, but Sean was on me just as I regained my balance, and before I knew it we were grappling on the slick stones. We were pretty evenly matched, and it probably looked like we were slow-dancing instead of wrestling. Mike and Budge tried to separate us, but before they could, we fell on the slippery rocks. That stunned us. We slowly got to our feet, painfully clutching different parts of our anatomies. My left elbow throbbed, and I could see that it was already turning purple. Mom would love that.

Sean limped away without a word, Mike helping him. Mike looked back over his shoulder and gave us an apologetic look as if to say, *Hey, I tried to stop him, but he's crazy. Don't blame me.*

I sat down on the grass and rubbed my elbow.

"What a jerk," Budge said, sitting down beside me.

"Who?"

"Sean, of course," Budge said.

My parents were still at work when I got home, so I was able to change out of my wet clothes without any questions. But there was nothing I could do about the purple bruise on my elbow. Sure enough, when Mom came home, the first words out of her mouth were, "What did you do to your elbow?"

"I fell," I said, which was true, even if Sean had helped gravity.

"Did you ice it?" She gently turned my arm so she could get a better look at the bruise. I nodded, even though I had forgotten to do that. "Nothing's broken, but that's going to hurt for a while."

When Dad saw it, though, *his* first question was, "Were you in a fight?"

"No."

He took my chin in his hand and lifted my head up. "Look me in the eyes and tell me that."

"I mean, yes." I could never lie to him eye to eye.

Dad sighed and released my chin. "Aren't you too old to be getting into fights?"

"I guess, but it wasn't much of a fight, more like a shoving contest."

"I don't care, Hay, it's all the same. What was it about?" I told him and made sure he understood that I wasn't the one who started it. "Maybe not, but it takes two," he said.

Jeezul. Philosophy. I hated it when he did that.

"You know better."

"Yeah, I guess," I said.

"Son, the world is full of loud mouths," Dad said. "If you go around taking swings at every one you meet, you'll never have time to do anything else."

"But Sean's a jerk."

"So's his father." Dad grinned. "But that's just the way it is. Ignore people like that. They're not worth your time or energy. You don't see me wasting time watching the jerks on Fox News, do you?"

"No."

"No, and I don't waste my time with fools either. Trust me, they're not worth it."

"Okay, Dad," I said, "I got it."

"Alright. Good boy." He tousled my hair. "You're grounded tomorrow."

3

B EING GROUNDED MEANT I would be spending Saturday at
Dad's auto repair shop on Karl Brown Way. He specializes in
foreign cars—what he calls *exotic cars*—but his garage is so small
he can't work on more than two cars at a time. I like hanging out
at the shop. Dad knows it, so his grounding me wasn't much of a
punishment at all. I think he knows that, too. I help him with little
tasks, but most of the time I watch him work and we talk as he
works.

He loves tinkering around with anything mechanical, but he
hasn't had the shop all that long. I remember—but barely because I
was little then—when he was still teaching history at the high school.
He loves history as much as he loves playing around with tools, and
he has a degree in American history from Ohio University. He may
love history, but he did not love teaching, so, when a favorite uncle
died and left him a little money, he quit teaching and opened the
shop. It doesn't have a name; people just call it "Ron's Place."

Dad had a 1985 Mercedes jacked up. He was on his back under the car, draining the oil out of it. I sat on the floor beside him, handing him tools as he asked for them.

The weather was still warm. The garage door was open to the street. There wasn't much traffic because the street was a dead-end at Nisbet Park. We could see the park amphitheater from the shop window. A guy all decked out in red and green Spandex whizzed by on a bike, heading for the trail along the river. I like bikes. I hate Spandex.

"Hand me that wrench again, will you?" Dad said, reaching out a greasy hand from beneath the car. "Thanks."

I don't know how he got on the subject, but somehow Dad was talking about the battle of Gettysburg. A Smith relative had fought there in a Pennsylvania regiment. He got shot but survived the war. Dad knew everything there was to know about Gettysburg and the Civil War and he was telling me the story for about the zillionth time. I was only half-listening to him, but it got me to thinking.

"Hey, Dad?" I said, interrupting his story.

"Hmm?"

"Do you think you'll be called up?"

He didn't answer right away. I heard the wrench turning on something and then he said, "It's a possibility, I suppose. You don't get a whole lot of warning."

"Would you go?"

He slid out from under the Benz. "Well, it's not like I would have a choice but, yes, I'd go. That's my job, Hay. I'm not saying I'd like it, but I would go."

There were things I wanted to ask him, like, did he think he would be in danger, was he afraid to go, stuff like that, but I didn't know how to ask those questions without sounding like a wimp. I didn't want it to seem like I was wondering about those things, even if I was.

"Let's not worry about it until the time comes," Dad said, "if it comes. No sense in upsetting your mother needlessly."

Yeah, we don't want to upset Mom.

We didn't hear anything more about his unit being deployed, so things went pretty much back to normal, although I could see Mom was still worried. Her work as an environmental technician keeps her busy, though, and I know city council stuff makes her crazy, so she doesn't have a lot of time to think about it. And Dad is Dad; he keeps things to himself.

As for me, soccer was starting up again and I was eager to play. Budge doesn't play. In fact, he doesn't play any sports at all. Sure, he'll shoot some baskets now and then, but to my knowledge he's never actually played a game of basketball in his life, and he never joins any sports teams. He says his dad, Merv, won't let him, because he has a hole in his heart, whatever that's supposed to mean.

The Loveland Braves practice a couple times a week in the early evening and play on the weekends. Dad sometime helps at practice. He's never played soccer but at least he knows the rules of the game, which is more than a lot of other parents know. I'm a striker. Last year I scored the second highest number of goals in the season. This year, I was shooting for number one.

When I'm not playing soccer, I hang out with Budge. There are some other guys that hang with us sometimes, too, but I can always count on Budge to be there.

One day after school, we were at his house watching *Ghost Hunters.* His parents were at work and the only other person at home was his sister Susan—at nine years old, the baby in their family. She walked into the room where Budge and I were watching TV, Jason and Grant stumbling around in the dark of some old, spooky mansion. She stopped short and glared at her brother, hands on her hips like a little mother.

"I'm telling, Budge," she said.

He waved his fingers at her as if he was shooing away a pesky fly.

"What's she talking about?" I asked.

He shook his head. "Nothing."

His sister didn't give up. "You're not supposed to watch that stuff. Daddy said."

"Suzie, why don't you call yourself outside to play?" His eyes remained fixed on the TV. "Oh, I've seen this one." He picked up the remote.

She stomped her foot. "You're going to be in big trouble when I tell Daddy!" She stormed off, ponytail bouncing.

"Jeezul-Pete, what's her problem?"

Budge sighed. "My dad's not big on ghost programs."

"Why not?"

"He says all that stuff is the work of the devil. He says no good Christian should have anything to do with ghosts, even if they're only on TV."

"Really?" I had never heard anyone say that before. He nodded. "Will your sister get you in trouble?"

"Snoopy Suzie? Nah, it'll be my word against hers and I'm older." He started surfing through the channels, only because it turned out we had both seen that episode and thought it was boring.

"Budge, what's your dad mean when he says that ghosts are devils?"

"I'm really not sure," he said.

"So, do you believe that?"

"That ghosts are devils?" He turned to me, the remote pointing at the TV like a gun. "I don't know. Maybe they could be. Maybe not devils, like with horns and all that, but maybe evil spirits of some kind."

"Maybe, but I doubt it," I said. "I mean, if a ghost is supposed to be the spirit of a person that was once alive, let's say your great-grandfather or someone like that, what would suddenly turn him into an evil spirit? If your great-grandfather was Osama bin Laden, okay, maybe then I could see it, but if not, it's still just your great-grandfather, wouldn't you think?"

"That's more how I think about ghosts, too. I don't believe they're evil," said Budge.

"But your dad does."

"He says it's in the Bible."

"But that doesn't automatically make it true," I said.

"It does for some people. You know, we should go back to the castle," he said, clearly trying to change the conversation.

I let him. "You think so? Why?"

"I don't know. It's just such a cool place," he said.

"You think it's got ghosts?"

"I asked *you* that once, remember? You said you didn't think so."

"If I remember, Budge, I said I didn't think there were any ghost *knights* there, since it wasn't a real castle, but I didn't say there might not be some other ghosts there. Maybe the guy that built it. He was kind of a weird old guy."

"Yeah, I heard that, too," Budge said.

"What about your father? What would he do if he found out?"

"He's not going to find out."

"Okay," I said, "it's your neck."

Budge is a quiet kid and it surprised me he was willing to cross his father like that. He must really love ghosts, more than I thought. Or maybe he's hot on them just because his father is so much against them.

Inspired by TV, we decided to spend the night at the castle to do some ghost hunting. We used the oldest trick in the book to get our parents' permission. We lied. We told them we were camping out in the back yard of another kid, a real smart guy named Frank Corona. All the parents loved Frank—he was intelligent and polite—so they didn't bother to check with his parents to see if we really *were* camping out at the Corona house. I was surprised it worked. Surely, when our parents were kids, they must have pulled the same stunt on *their* parents. Did they forget?

In any case, on a Friday night we lugged sleeping bags and backpacks down to the castle on our bikes. We couldn't have asked for a better night. It was early September, and the nights hadn't yet gotten too cold. The sleeping bags would be fine. A full moon reflected off the river and our shadows walked along the bank beside us.

Sometimes, one of the Knights stays overnight at the castle, I guess to guard the place, but there were no cars when we arrived. As near as we could tell, we were alone. That still didn't mean we could get inside, though. We couldn't break through the heavy wooden door, even if we had wanted to. The door was thick as a brick and studded with hundreds of iron nails. Not that it wouldn't have been way cool to spend the night inside the castle, but breaking and entering was pushing things a little too far.

We left our bikes beside the stonewall below the castle, hiding them in the bushes. A large archway opened onto the grounds of the castle, where twin towers of the central building rose against the hillside. To the right was a long, two-story wing rounded at the end. To the left of the castle were the gardens, set among stone terraces that climbed the hill.

We dropped our gear with the bikes while we went exploring.

Our shadows staggered like drunks against the walls of the castle rising high above us. The many narrow windows were like dark eyes looking down on us. It was not hard to believe that someone was standing inside, watching.

"Can you imagine spending your whole life working on this thing, like Sir Harry did?"

"No way. It's crazy," Budge said. We had come to the place where the wing angled off from the main building. The moonlight didn't reach there. We were in darkness. "Do you suppose he's still here?"

"Sir Harry? I don't know. Let's find out." Raising my voice, I called, "Sir Harry, are you here?"

"Don't do that!" Even in the dark I could see Budge's eyes darting around.

"Harry, if you're here, will you show yourself?"

"I mean it, Hay."

"But that's what they do on TV. All the ghosthunters do that. They call the ghost and ask it to do something, or talk to them," I said.

"Yeah, I know."

"So?"

"It makes me nervous is all," said Budge.

"Okay, let's just check around a little bit more."

"Good."

He sounded relieved.

We walked through the arches of the stables and here, too, it was mostly darkness. This was where I thought I had heard someone laughing the last time we were there. I hurried us through. We came out behind the castle and hiked over to the terraced gardens at the other side, coming out at their highest point on the hillside. The Knights of the Golden Trail liked to garden and the terraces were filled with plants and flowers of all kinds, even though some were already fading as fall was coming on. By the light of the moon, the stalks and branches waving in the breeze from the river looked like skinny ghosts.

We carefully made our way down the terrace until we were back at the riverside where we had left our bikes and gear.

"Where do you want to set up?" I said.

"What about the garden?"

The garden seemed as good a place as any. Secretly, I was glad he didn't suggest the stables. "Fine, let's go." I picked up my pack and sleeping bag.

We climbed back to the third-level terrace where we found a spot large enough for us to roll out our sleeping bags. I dropped my pack on the bag. "What kind of equipment did you bring?"

"I got a camera and a recorder," Budge said, "and I brought my *Ghosthunting Ohio* book."

"Cool," I said. "I've got my dad's old camcorder and I also have this." I dug in my bag and pulled out a board printed with numbers and letters and the words "yes," "no," and "goodbye."

Budge's eyes went wide. "Jeezul-Pete! You didn't."

"What?"

"That's a Ouija board."

"Pretty sure I knew that Budge."

"Are you planning on using that thing here?"

"Well, yeah, that was kind of the general idea," I said.

He looked around nervously as though looking for a way to escape. "I'm not sure we should do that."

"Come on, Budge. We've seen people on TV use them all the time to connect with spirits."

"But they know what they're doing, Hay. We don't. They're trained professionals. We don't even have a ghosthunting learner's permit."

"Are you afraid?"

"Are you?"

Oh, snap! We looked at each other for a few moments, mentally tossing our challenges back and forth like a volleyball. I broke first. "Okay, maybe a little. But what if this thing really works, Budge? Wouldn't that be awesome?" He slowly nodded. "Let's try it, dude. Come on."

I reached into the bag again and took out the planchette, a heart-shaped piece of plastic with three little legs and a needle pointing down from a round window in the center. "Ready?"

I set the board on the ground and Budge dragged himself closer. "I didn't even know you had a Ouija board," he grumbled.

"We'll be fine, Budge, trust me."

He snorted. "Famous last words."

We sat with the board between us, the planchette in the center.

"Just a light touch," I said, as I leaned in and placed my fingers on one side of the planchette. Budge placed his on the opposite side. "Now ask a question."

Budge screwed up his face, concentrating, his eyes closed. He looked like he was in pain.

"Tonight, dude," I said.

"Right, got it." He opened his eyes. "Does Ama Yendi like Haycorn?"

I sat up. "Jeezul, Budge."

He looked up at me. "That's a question, isn't it? You said, 'ask a question.'"

"Yeah, but I didn't mean a stupid question," I said.

"Are we going to do it or not?"

"Fine." My turn to grumble.

We placed our fingers back on the planchette and Budge repeated the question. We stared at the planchette and then felt it give a little jerk. It started to spider-creep across the board, headed for "yes." *Oh, man!* But then it gave another jerk and reversed course, picking up speed until it came to "goodbye" where it stopped. We kept our fingers on the planchette, waiting to see if it would move again but it didn't. The answer to Budge's question was "goodbye."

"So, what's that supposed to mean?" Budge said.

"It means you're a blockhead," I said. "Now, if we're going to go through with this, we need to get serious. We're investigating ghosts, remember? Let me give it a shot." We reset the planchette in the center of the board. "Are there any spirits with us here tonight?"

All was quiet as we kept our eyes glued to the planchette. Nothing. We waited. I could hear Budge breathing. An owl hooted, startling my fingers off the planchette. I quickly placed them back on. Then, a vibration, a tug, as the planchette began to move again.

"Whoa ..." said Budge.

The planchette slid across the letters on the board and stopped at "H". It lingered there for only a few seconds before moving on. It hesitated when it reached "O", but did not stop. It continued, stopping at "A".

"Ha?" said Budge.

I shook my head. "That doesn't make sense, I'll try again. Are there any spirits in the castle?"

Surprisingly, the planchette moved again, retracing the same route as before.

"It's going crazy," said Budge.

Once again, the planchette spelled "HA" before coming to rest.

"Ha, ha? It's laughing at us," said Budge.

I sat back. "Hmm, seems like it, unless … wait a minute, Budge. What if those aren't words? What if they're initials?"

"Initials?"

"Yes! H.A. as in Harry Andrews!"

"Oh, my … Jeezul-Pete, Haycorn! We just discovered a ghost!"

4

WE WERE PUMPED! Did we have a ghost?

We didn't know the best way to do our investigation, but we couldn't wait to get started, so we walked around awhile taking pictures and shooting video. On the TV shows, the ghosthunters sometimes see things in the pictures or videos after they were recorded and reviewed, things they didn't see with the naked eye at the time. The TV guys called them *anomalies*. Sometimes, they looked like balls of light—*orbs*—sometimes like streaks, or clouds, or mist, but they were always weird. They were supposed to be spirit energy. If you were lucky you might see a person's face or even a whole body in the picture. That would be awesome. Budge took a lot of pictures. I kept the camcorder rolling for a while, hoping we would hit the jackpot later.

He turned on his digital voice recorder and tucked it into his shirt pocket, letting it record as we walked around. Just like the pictures, sometimes a recorder would pick up voices or sounds the ghosthunters didn't hear at the time. EVPs, they were called. That stood for electronic voice phenomena. Those were the voices of ghosts.

We kept at it for maybe an hour but then we started getting tired. "How much more space do you have on the recorder?"

He took it out of his pocket and held it close to see it now that the full moon had drifted further away. "Not sure, but I think I've got plenty yet. Why?"

"I was thinking we'd just put it somewhere in the castle and let it run."

"We could do that. Where's a good place?"

I hated to say it, but if we really wanted to find a ghost we had to go where the ghosts might be. "I never told you, but the last time we were here, when we had that run-in with the groundhog in the stable?"

"Yeah?"

"I could have sworn I heard a laugh as we left."

He looked at me bug-eyed. "Really? Then we should definitely set it up in the stable."

"I guess so." I tried to sound cool about it.

"Okay, let's go then," he said.

"Okay."

"Okay."

"You're not moving," I said.

"Neither are you."

"Together, then, alright?"

The trees at the top of the hill blocked the moonlight so our path to the stables was mostly in darkness. I had a small flashlight in my pocket that I turned on so we wouldn't trip over anything in the dark. It would be hard to explain a broken ankle to Mom, especially when I was supposed to be spending the night in the safety of Frank Corona's back yard. *Grounded for life* echoed in my head. That's a long time.

I noticed we were dragging our feet the closer we got to the stables.

"What do you think? Close enough?"

I kept thinking about that crazy Ouija board, but we had work to do. I swallowed my fear. "No, inside the stable. Come on, Budge."

"I thought you'd say that."

We entered through the arch into the stable. I ran the flashlight over the stone walls and found a little space in one of the arch's supporting columns about six feet above the ground. "There, that looks good," I said, keeping the light trained on the spot while Budge reached up and tucked the recorder in it.

Once he had done that we didn't waste any time getting out. Back in the garden, we sat on our sleeping bags, talking. With the warm night all around us, the place just didn't seem spooky. Maybe we'd find out it wasn't haunted after all. On the other hand, you never knew.

I guess we fell asleep. The next thing I knew something woke me up. Maybe a sound, I don't know, but my eyes were open and staring into the darkness. A weird prickly feeling tickled the back of my neck.

"Hey, Budge," I whispered, shaking him, "wake up." He mumbled something and rolled onto his side, but I shook him again. "Wake up, dude!"

I couldn't see the moon anymore, so it was pretty dark as I lay there looking down at Budge, who was stirring beside me.

"What's the matter?" he asked.

"I don't know. Something woke me up. Do you see anything?"

"No. Use your flashlight."

I didn't want to do that, afraid that if something was out there, and I had no idea what that something might be—a ghost maybe, who knew? —the light would give us away and I wasn't sure I wanted to *see* whatever it might be. Suddenly, a ray of pale light flared in the distance. It lit up the riverbank for a second, then was gone. Before I could say anything to Budge, it was back again, this time moving down the castle drive, heading toward the river.

Budge nudged me. "Is that a car?"

What could have been taken for two ghost orbs clearly became the headlights of a car slowly coming down the hill to the castle. In the darkness, everything looked gray. I couldn't tell what kind of car it was or even its color. It came to a stop in the castle driveway just beyond the gate, less than a hundred yards from where we lay hugging the ground as best we could. I didn't know what was going through Budge's mind, but I was wishing with all my heart I could disappear underground like our friendly castle groundhog.

The car's lights went out. We heard the door open.

"Oh, crap!" Budge said.

We didn't move, I don't think we breathed. I could feel my heart hammering against the ground. A dark figure emerged from the car and walked toward the stables. It was too dark to make out any details, but I was sure it was a man. He was carrying something, and all I could think was, *chainsaw.* As he drew closer, I could see the chainsaw was actually a metal case of some kind. He stopped short of the stables and then, a darker shadow emerged from beneath the arch and walked toward him. Where had he come from? The two men stood together for a few moments, no more than two black shadows, before entering the stables.

"W-what do we do now?" Budge said, looking like he might turn rabbit.

"Jeezul, Budge, how would I know?"

"Make a run for it?"

"When was the last time you outran a car? Look, they don't know we're here. Maybe if we're quiet and stay put we can wait them out."

And that's what we did. We lay still and didn't move a muscle. You would have thought we were dead. We didn't know how much time passed. Neither of us wanted to check the time on our cell phones—or make a call for that matter—afraid the glow from the phone would be like a spotlight on our position. My heart pounded against the earth like a pile driver. I bet Budge's was doing the same, even if it did have a hole in it. We were so afraid that it never even occurred to us to grab our cameras and take some pictures. My hands were shaking so badly, I wouldn't have been able to hold the phone steady anyway. And I had to pee. After a while—I don't know how long—the two men came out from the stables, one of them carrying the metal case.

The driver got back into his car, without the case. In the few seconds that the car's interior lights were on, I caught a glimpse of him. A tall, bald guy with a moustache. The door closed, the headlights switched on and the car slowly made its way back up the castle drive. The man with the case watched the car drive away before heading back to the stables. He was there for some time, but we had no idea what he was doing. Finally, he came out and began walking toward the river. By the riverbank it was nothing but blackness. I lost sight of him.

"Can you still see him?"

"No," said Budge, "too dark."

We heard scraping sounds from the river, something being dragged over rocks, and then hollow clunking sounds that we recognized, the sound someone makes stepping into a canoe. I wasn't certain—it could be my ears playing tricks on me—but I thought I heard the *shush* of his canoe cutting the water.

Everything was quiet now at the castle, but we still waited awhile before cautiously gathering our gear and making our way down the terrace. By then, the sky was turning a pearly gray color. It was clear that no one else was at the castle. We hurried down to our bikes and tied our gear to them. The river flowed by. There was no one there.

"Oh, Jeezul! The recorder!" Budge said.

We went back to the stables, neither one of us wanting to separate from the other. Gray light now seeped in beneath the arches as early morning came on.

"It's still there." I reached up to get it. "Now let's get out of here."

It was almost dawn by the time I got home. I was so exhausted, I barely had time to pull off my clothes before my head hit the pillow and I was down for the count. The next day was Saturday and I slept in. By the time I finally opened my eyes the sun was streaming in through the window, shining on my Lionel Messi poster, his face glowing like a god. Birds were chirping outside the window. I heard Mrs. Schaefer's insane pug barking at nothing again. I lay there thinking about the previous night, and my mind filled with a million questions: who were those guys? What were they doing? What was in the briefcase? I knew Budge and I would have to go back to the castle to investigate. I also knew we shouldn't tell anyone anything just yet.

It was surprisingly quiet in the house for a Saturday morning. I looked at the clock beside my bed. Ten-thirty. I got up, threw on jeans and a T-shirt and shuffled out of my bedroom. I walked into the kitchen and there were Mom and Dad sitting across from each other at the table. They each had a mug of coffee, but neither of them was drinking. From the stony expressions on their faces, I knew something was up, and it wasn't good.

Dad looked up, "Hey, son." *Son* was his serious name for me.

"Hi, Dad." Mom didn't look at me. "So, what's up?"

"Well." He slowly rubbed his palms together, a nervous tic of his. "It seems like my unit is finally being called up."

Even though I knew I might hear those words from him some time, they hit me like a slap. I pulled out a chair and sat down. "When?"

"In a week."

Mom looked at me and I could see that she had been crying. "We'll have to get ready for when Dad leaves."

I wasn't exactly sure what she meant by that. Stupidly, all I could think was that he would miss our soccer game against the first place Titans ten days from now.

"Okay."

"There will be time to get everything sorted out before I go," Dad said.

"Okay."

He seemed embarrassed, as though he had done something wrong but, of course, he hadn't. "Don't worry, Hay."

"Okay." I realized I was repeating myself, but I didn't know what else to say. This was all new to me.

Mom stood up and took her mug to the sink. She dumped the cold coffee down the drain and turned to me. "Do you want me to make you some eggs for breakfast?" She tried on a lopsided smile.

I wasn't hungry. "Yes," I said, "please."

5

I DON'T WANT TO TALK ABOUT what that week was like before Dad left. He and Mom spent a lot of time talking about I don't know what, looking through papers from their file box, writing things down, stuff like that. We all tried to act normal, like maybe Dad wasn't really going, there had been some mistake. But the day one of Dad's Army buddies came by to pick him up—Dad already dressed in his BDU, his battle dress uniform—was the worst day in my life. I'm sure Mom felt the same. So, that's all I want to say about that week.

I mean, I had a million questions I wanted to ask Dad, but was afraid to hear the answers: how long would he be gone? Where exactly would he be in Afghanistan? Doing what? Most of all, would he be safe? There was a good chance that Dad would do what parents always did when they didn't want their kids to worry about something serious—downplay it with a smile and, if the kids were little, maybe an ice cream cone—so I knew there was no point in asking my questions. I dragged them around inside me like river rocks.

So, yeah, it was a rough week.

No surprise then, that I hadn't given much thought to going back to the castle, but after we got a couple emails from Dad telling us that he was alright, I started wondering again about what Budge and I had seen that night. He had been thinking about it, too.

"What do you think was in that briefcase?" Budge asked one day, as we rode the bus home from school.

"I don't know. In the movies, they're always filled with money."

He nodded. "Yeah, that's what I was thinking. But it could have been a bomb or something like that. Maybe the guys were terrorists."

"Shh, quiet!" I looked around at the other kids on the bus, but no one seemed interested in listening to what we were saying. Most of them were wearing earbuds and were lost in their own little worlds. "Let's keep this thing to ourselves. We should go back," I said, almost whispering.

"I wish we knew who those guys were and what they were talking about."

"Yeah, me too." Suddenly, I remembered. "Wait a minute. We had that recorder going in the stables. Did you listen to it?"

He looked at me as if I had just grown two heads. "No, I haven't. I wanted to, but Merv had me doing some chores with him and my sisters gave me no privacy. But, Hay, we might have recorded them!"

I grinned. "Yep, maybe."

As soon as the bus dropped us off, we ran to Budge's house. We shrugged off our backpacks and let them fall to the floor. His sister Susan was already home from school, and she gave us the fish-eye but didn't follow us, content to mutter something about *stupid Budge* as we scooted by her to his bedroom. We locked the door just in case.

He took the recorder down from a shelf and we sat on the floor with it. Keeping the volume down low so that a certain someone who was probably listening at the door couldn't hear, we leaned close and listened.

For a while, all we heard was our footsteps and aimless chatter as we walked around the castle.

"You sound like a chipmunk on that thing," I said.

Budge didn't answer. Some scraping sounds came from the recorder and then it was silent. For a long time.

I don't know how the ghost guys on TV do it, listening to hours and hours of recordings. *Boring* isn't a strong enough word to describe it. We lay there on the floor for at least an hour listening to nothing. One time we heard an owl hoot, but then nothing more.

"This is ridiculous. How long do you think it recorded?"

"No idea," Budge said.

"Great."

I sat up and stretched. Just then, we heard some noises on the recorder. I looked at Budge. He was staring at the recorder as if he could see the sounds coming from it. "Tires. On gravel."

"Yes. There's the car door and footsteps," I said

We heard people walking and then voices, close to the recorder. My ears felt like they were growing larger as I leaned in to listen.

Where's your car? a man's voice said, *I didn't see it.*

It doesn't matter. Do you have it? the second man asked.

Of course. Right here. One hundred grand in the hand.

Open it, the second man said, *I want to see it.*

There was something about the second man's voice that seemed familiar to me, as though I had heard it before somewhere. Maybe it was an accent, I didn't know, but it nagged at me.

We heard what sounded like metal snaps or locks coming undone and then someone giving out a low whistle. Then the second man spoke again.

Nice, he said. *You must really want that velodrome if you're willing to part with all that money.*

"Budge! Is that Mr. Davenport?"

"The mayor?"

"Stop. Play it again," I said.

He replayed it and we both listened carefully to the second man.

"That sure sounds like the mayor, doesn't it?"

"I guess," said Budge. He turned off the recorder. "I'm not sure what he sounds like."

"I've heard him at city council meetings. He's got this sort of I'm-better-than-you way of talking. I bet that's Mr. Davenport!"

"Okay, suppose it is him. What's he doing? Who's the other guy?"

"I don't know," I said, "but if someone is handing you one hundred thousand dollars in some lonely place in the middle of the night—and you're the mayor, by the way—it's probably something illegal, wouldn't you think? Here, turn the recorder back on. Let's see if there's anything more."

He switched it on, and we listened intently.

I've got my reasons, the first man said.

Makes no difference to me, the second man said—I was sure now that it was Mr. Davenport—*I got what I wanted.*

I felt something in the pit of my stomach, almost like I was going to be sick. Whatever we had heard, it wasn't good. That much was clear. And now that we had heard it, were we in trouble? I mean, Mr. Davenport ran the city. What would happen to us if he knew we had recorded him?

We heard the first man say something on the recorder, but it was garbled and we couldn't make out the words. We heard footsteps crunching on the gravel and then, a whispery, raspy voice, completely different from the other two, said, *Leave me.* The voice sent a chill through me. "Whoa, what was that?"

Budge was looking at me, bug-eyed. "No idea, man," he said. He replayed the recorder. "*Leave me* is what I heard. Jeezul, that's a creepy voice!"

"I heard the same thing. Who *is* that?"

"It wasn't either of the two guys, that's for sure," Budge said.

"Was there someone else there? Someone we didn't see?"

"You mean someone like a ghost?" said Budge.

We looked at each other as if we had just seen that ghost. Words failed us. The ghosthunter guys on TV would sometimes get voices like that on their recorders and they knew they were ghost voices. Now we had captured one, too!

"That is awesome," I said.

Budge nodded. "Oh, yeah."

But after a few moments my excitement faded as I thought again of the two men, the two flesh-and-blood men. I may have been a kid, but I wasn't stupid. Whatever went down that night between Mayor Davenport and the mystery man was more than fishy. Someone needed to know about it; maybe Mom could figure out what it was all about. But how did I explain having the recording without admitting that I had spent the night at the castle? Without permission. She seemed more irritable these days with Dad gone and I really didn't want to be grounded again. Still, she needed to hear the recording.

I thought maybe if I had Budge with me when I told her, she wouldn't be so mad. It was worth a shot, even though Budge was not thrilled about the idea.

We were sitting in the living room when she got home from work. She took one look at us sitting there on the couch like bookends and knew something was up.

"Please don't tell me you've been expelled from school," Mom said, dropping her purse on the coffee table.

"No."

"And the police won't be dropping by to talk to me about you?"

"No, Mom!"

"Okay, that's a relief." She sat in the rocker across from us. "So, what kind of trouble *are* you two in?"

"Mom, if I lied to you about something, but then I found out something really important because I lied to you and then told you about it, would you be mad because I lied to you in the first place? Would you ground me?"

Budge stared at me like I was an idiot.

"Hay, I really don't have time for this. I've got a lot on my mind right now," Mom said, wearily. I knew I was pushing her buttons, but I couldn't help it. "Just tell me what's going on," she said.

I took a breath. "Okay, remember that night Budge and I stayed over at Frank's?" She nodded. "Well, we didn't. We went to the castle instead."

She frowned and I saw that Snake-Eye face beginning to show. "Go on," she said.

"So, I lied to you."

"I got that part, Haycorn. Go on with your story."

"We were ghost hunting at the castle. We had a recorder with us, and we left it in the castle, but then we saw two men there."

Mom raised an eyebrow. "Two men?"

Wait, the ghost part didn't surprise her?

"We think one of them was Mr. Davenport," Budge blurted out. I shot him a look. Timing was everything with Mom.

She stopped rocking and leaned forward in the chair. "The mayor?"

"It sounds like his voice on the recorder," I said.

"The recorder. You recorded the mayor at the castle? In the middle of the night?" There was the full Snake-Eye. "You better tell me everything, Haycorn, and don't leave anything out."

So, we did. When we had finished, she sat there like I had hit her with a board. Finally, she said, "I'll have to keep that recorder until I can download it to my computer."

"Sure, Mom, whatever you need," I said, politely. After all, she had not yet said anything about being grounded.

She took the recorder and walked into the study where she worked on all her city council stuff. She closed the door behind her.

"What do you think your mom's going to do?" Budge said. He had that worried look I had seen so often in him.

"I don't know, but she's smart. She'll figure out what it's all about."

He nodded. "Okay. Sorry, Hay, I've got to get going. If I'm late for dinner, Merv will kill me."

Merv is what he called his dad—not to his face, of course.

He stood. "Dude! What about the ghost voice?"

42

"Maybe she won't hear it," I said.

"Fat chance." He walked to the front door. "How can she miss it?"

"You may be right. I hope she doesn't freak out. There's nothing we can do about it now."

"Let me know how it goes," he said, as he left the house.

It wasn't much later that Mom came out from the study. "I made a copy on my computer, but I'm going to hold on to the recorder. I don't think you guys should be running around town with it."

"It belongs to Budge."

"Fine, I've got one you can use in the meantime if you need it. I don't know if you understand what was happening on that recording, Haycorn, but I want you to promise me that you won't tell anyone about it. Budge must promise, too."

"What *was* going on?"

She frowned. "I can't say right now. I need to be certain of some things, but I will tell you once I know everything for sure. But promise me, Haycorn. This could be dangerous."

Her eyes drilled into me. She wasn't fooling around. "I promise," I said.

"And Budge?"

"Don't worry, he'll listen to me." At least I hoped he would. Sometimes, Budge just didn't get it.

"Okay." She still hadn't said anything about grounding me, so I was hopeful that she had not thought about it, but when she looked at me with a quizzical expression on her face, I thought I was in for it. "Hay," she said, "I thought you said there were two men at the castle that night."

"Yes, that's right. Two."

"But there was a third voice on the recorder. Who was that?"

6

W OW, *WHERE TO BEGIN!* "You better sit down, Mom."
"I am sitting."

She was, but I had always wanted to say that line. I came close the time I accidentally shot-put a brick through Mister Olenski's windshield—I was never very good at track and field—but didn't say it.

I sat down on the couch. "Mom, do you believe in ghosts?"

"Ghosts? As in, sheet-wearing, chain-rattling, spirits of the dead?" I nodded. "No, at least not like that."

"What do you mean?"

"Where are you going with this, Haycorn?" A question she often asked me.

"That voice on the recorder, that third guy? We never saw a third person."

"You're saying it was a ghost?"

"We think so."

She stopped rocking. "Hmm." She looked up at the ceiling, thinking, and then looked at me. "I don't believe in the Hollywood, *Ghostbusters* kind of ghost, but I do think there's the possibility we go on in some form after we die. That's hard for me to say. As a scientist, I should rely only on proof, but how do you prove an afterlife? I can't explain it any better than that, but I think it's possible."

Mom was a scientist. Facts and proof were what mattered to her. There wasn't much room in her science for ghosts. Still, she had admitted to the possibility that there might be some kind of life after death, and there wasn't anything scientific about that. Maybe it was just hope.

"So do we, me and Budge," I said, excitedly—Mom was a believer! "We think we caught a ghost on the recorder. Just like on TV."

"That's entertainment, Hay; I wouldn't be so quick to trust everything I saw on television."

"I don't, but the recorder is proof, wouldn't you say?"

She was rocking again. "Proof of ghosts? I doubt it would stand up in a court of law."

"Yeah, I guess all we can really prove is that we recorded a third voice, right? I mean, we didn't see the speaker," I said.

"Right," said Mom. "For all you know, a third person *could* have been there, hidden from your view."

She was bumming me out. "So, you don't believe it was a ghost."

She smiled. "I'm not saying that. All I'm saying is, it's hard to prove."

I was quiet for a while, studying the floor, noticing a dust bunny that had rolled beneath the coffee table.

"Don't look so glum, Sweetie. I'm not saying you didn't record a ghost. Listen, did I ever tell you my ghost story?"

I perked up. "You have a ghost story? You never told me."

"Yes, it happened when I was in college. I shared a dorm room with another girl. She slept in the bottom bunk, and I slept up top. One night I woke up and saw a man standing in our room."

46

"A man? That must have freaked you out," I said.

"There was a full moon shining through the window, so there was some light to see by and I could clearly see the figure of the man. It was my Grandpa Joe, my mother's father."

"How did you know? Did he talk to you?"

"No, he never said a word. The funny thing was I couldn't see the details of his face all that well," said Mom. "But somehow I knew it was Grandpa Joe and that he was there just to check up on me to see how I was doing."

I was sitting on the edge of the couch. "What did you do then?"

Mom laughed. "Nothing. I rolled over and went back to sleep."

"Really?"

"You know what was so odd, though? Grandpa Joe died when I was little, maybe two or three years old. I hardly knew him. I don't remember seeing a lot of pictures of him lying around our house. And yet, I knew with certainty the man was Grandpa Joe. Isn't that strange?"

It *was* strange. But the TV ghost guys always had someone on their team who could see ghosts. I don't know how those people did it; something they were born with, I guess. They seemed like normal people, just normal people who could see dead people. They seemed as normal as ... Mom. "You're psychic, Mom!"

"Oh, sure," she said, with a laugh. "Psychic as a rock."

She was wrong. I had read enough to know that she must have some psychic powers to see a ghost, even if she didn't know she had them. One of my favorite books is *Ghosthunters*. It talks about how we all have psychic powers, but only a few of us know how to use them. Maybe Mom is like that, with unknown powers.

"But that's not all. I had an incident that involved you when you were a baby."

"Jeezul-Pete! Me?" I was all ears again.

"When you were a little over one-year-old, you woke me up with your crying. You didn't cry too much at that age and mostly slept through the night, but this time you were really carrying on, crying and screaming, so I got up to see what was wrong.

"You were standing in your crib, crying, staring at your closet door, which was open. I had stored the electric Christmas candles that we had placed in the windows of your room on the top shelf of the closet. The candles were turned on."

"What? Were they plugged in?"

"No, this happened in July," Mom said.

"Oh, man! What did you do?"

"I looked at them glowing in the closet and thought, *well, that's weird* and then I brought you into my bed."

"That's all? You were pretty cool about it. A lot of people would pee their pants."

She looked thoughtful. "Yes, I guess I was pretty cool, but it's like my brain couldn't accept what it experienced, so it chose to ignore it, or brush it off as some electrical malfunction or something. Maybe it couldn't handle the truth."

"That it was a ghost?"

"If not a ghost, something highly unusual. I guess you would call it paranormal," she said.

"Definitely. All that word really means is something out of the normal. I think unplugged lights turning on by themselves would be freaking paranormal."

"So, do you have a ghost on the recorder or don't you? That's the question."

Yes, it was, and I was going to try to answer it one way or the other.

"But Haycorn," Mom continued, using my full name, which meant that I was either being grounded or she had seen my math grades, "I don't want you going back to the castle."

"What? Why not?"

"I just don't," she said.

"How will we do our research, Mom? Please?"

48

"I don't know," Mom said, "but you're not to go back to the castle. Period."

"Question mark," I said. "Why not?"

Mom's expression told me I was pushing my luck and I had the idea the floor would crumble beneath my feet if I wasn't careful.

"No means no, Haycorn. That's final."

Sure, easy for her to say.

•   •   •

Later, Mom got an email from Dad. He couldn't email us very often, so each one was a big deal. This one was a really big deal because he said that soon he would be able to get on Skype to talk with us, so not only would we hear him, but we would be able to see him too. That would be the first time since he left. I couldn't think about ghosts, or anything else. Dad hadn't been gone all that long, really, but it seemed like forever. I missed him.

We thought about him when we saw news stories about Afghanistan on TV. It was impossible not to. Dad couldn't give us the details about where he was or what he was doing, so every time we heard something about soldiers being killed over there, we wondered, was he there? Could that just as easily have been him? We never said anything to each other like that, but I'm pretty sure Mom thought those things. I know I did.

Several hours later we sat by the computer in the study watching the clock. Dad had given us a time when he thought he could call, and we were excited as we waited for him. Mom sat in the desk chair, anxiously tapping her fingers on the desk. I had pulled up an ottoman beside her. She smiled at me, but she looked nervous. The time difference between Ohio and Afghanistan was something like eight or nine hours so, while it was mid-morning here, it was evening there. We watched the monitor waiting for something to happen. Boring.

"What time did Dad say he would call?" I asked, while scrolling through Ama Yendi's Facebook timeline on my phone. No mention of me anywhere. Not that I expected to see one, but it would have been a nice surprise.

"He's late," she said.

There was a picture of Ama and some other girls at volleyball practice. Ama was looking right at the camera with a big smile on her face and it felt like she was smiling at me. I smiled back.

Finally, we heard the musical beeping of an incoming call.

"Hello, can you hear me?" Dad's voice came over the speakers before his picture came up on the monitor.

We both answered him at the same time. When his picture came up, the color was washed out a little and his movements were jerky, like an old-time movie.

"Not a great connection," I said. "This sucks."

"Haycorn! Watch your language," Mom said. "He's in Afghanistan. We're lucky we're even connected."

Dad was wearing his BDUs, and he looked tired, but okay. His face looked red, sun-burned. He never did tan well. The wall behind him was blank and over his left shoulder I could see what looked like the corner of a window.

"Sorry I'm late," Dad said. "Couldn't be helped. How are you two?"

"We're fine," Mom said. "How about you? How are you holding up?"

He grinned. "Oh, it's a picnic over here. Fresh air, plenty of sunshine, wonderful, friendly people ..."

"Really?" I said.

Mom frowned.

"Nothing but good times, Haycorn." I saw the arm of another soldier briefly appear at the edge of the screen. Dad looked up for a second and nodded.

"Everything okay at home, Anne?" he asked, turning his attention back to the camera.

"Yes, we're okay," Mom said, softly. "Don't worry about us."

He nodded, his lips pressed tightly together as if something was trying to escape from behind them. It was a weird expression I had never seen in him before. Then he seemed to brighten, and he said, "What about that game with the Rockets, Hay? How did you guys do?"

"Awesome, Dad. We really kicked their… I mean, we won, two-zip."

"No kidding? You shut them out? That *is* awesome."

"I scored one of the goals."

"Way to go, son. High five!" We pressed our hands to our monitors, and I could swear I actually felt his hand touch mine over all those miles and miles. It felt great.

"School going okay for you?"

"Sure, it's fine."

He nodded. "Okay." Then he looked serious again. "Hay, I don't have much time left on the call before we let someone else use the computer, so if it's okay with you, let me talk with your mom for a few minutes alone, okay?"

"Sure, Dad."

"Thanks, love you, buddy."

"Love you too, Dad."

I got up and left the room, closing the door behind me, leaving Mom alone with him.

I sat on the couch in the living room. Mom's voice behind the door was muffled. It was obvious she had lowered her voice to keep their talk private, and that was fine with me. I was just glad to hear his voice and to see him and to know that he was okay.

It was strange having Dad away from home like that. I thought about him a lot, but at the same time, there were stretches of time in which I didn't think about him. There was the ghost. Ama. Soccer. I mean, it wasn't like I was *trying* to forget about him, it just happened sometimes. And sometimes, I felt bad when that happened. Guilty in some way.

7

T UESDAY EVENING. City council night. Mom always dressed
up for council meetings because she believed that showed
respect for her office but mostly because the meetings were televised
over a local cable station. Mom looked like a lawyer, I thought, in
black skirt and jacket. She carried her official papers in a briefcase. I
have to give her credit. A few days before every meeting, a Loveland
police officer would come to the house and deliver a packet that
contained all the materials to be discussed at the upcoming meeting.
She read them all, every page, every word, her yellow Hi-Liter
working overtime. When you heard her speak at the meeting, it was
obvious she had done her homework. It was also obvious some of
the men had not, especially Mr. Baer, who usually sat there looking
smug, a little nervous tic jumping on his face when he was finally
called upon to say something.

"Do you want to go with me tonight, Hay?" Mom said.

Sure, as much as I wanted to run extra laps at soccer practice. I was really worn out from a particularly intense soccer practice after school. Coach Winslow had a bug up his butt about one of our recent losses and we paid for that in practice. He had us doing wind-sprints up and down the length of the field. I hated that. We all hated that. All I wanted now was to crash in front of the TV.

But I had been to a few meetings before. Mostly against my will. Sometimes they were fun, like the one they did every year where kids from the high school conducted the meeting as though they were city councilmen; that was always the bomb. The real council people would sit behind the kids, coaching them. It was like they were pulling the strings of those kid puppets. It wouldn't be any fun that night, I knew, but I was worried about Mom because of what we had heard on the recorder. Who knew what might happen at the meeting? I thought I should go with her.

And, Mom told me the girls from school who were doing stuff for the environment—we called them the Green Girls—would be there to make a presentation. That would mean Ama would be there. *Yeah*, I thought, *I should definitely go.*

Mom checked her watch. "Okay, brush your hair and put on a clean shirt. Be quick about it. I have to get going."

When we got to City Hall, I took a seat in the back of the room while Mom went up to her place at the long, curved council desk. The Loveland city seal—a big red heart, I swear—hung on the wall above the desk, flanked by US and Ohio flags.

Half a dozen or so girls sat up near the front. They were all wearing green T-shirts. I guessed they were uniforms, but I couldn't see if a logo or something was printed on them. I recognized most of the girls from school. One was Ama Yendi. She once told me that in Ghana, where she came from, people were often named after the day on which they were born. Her name meant she was born on Saturday. Ama had dark hair and dark eyes, and skin the color of coffee. She laughed a lot. I liked that.

Each meeting began with a public forum, and Ama and the other girls took their places at the podium, along with Ama's mother, who also wore a green t-shirt. One look at Mrs. Yendi's blue eyes and reddish-colored hair told you that Ama mostly inherited her Ghanaian father's genes. The podium was angled to one side, and I could see that each of the shirts had a large tree printed on the front. Ama tilted the microphone down to where she could reach it.

It turns out the girls had formed an environmental club, the Loveland Environmental something-or-other, and they had a project in mind for the East Loveland Nature Preserve. That place was near and dear to Mom's heart, since she had done so much to push for its creation. Anyway, the girls wanted to build a bird blind in the preserve. Really? The girls were going to build a bird blind? *That* I wanted to see.

"Would there be a cost to the city?" Mom smiled at Ama. I could see that she liked the idea.

"No, ma'am," Ama said.

Mrs. Yendi bent to the microphone. "We hope to get donations for the lumber and other building materials, and we'll supply the labor."

The mayor put down his newspaper. "You'll have to submit the building plans to the building inspector for approval."

Mom glared at him.

"Okay," Mrs. Yendi said, slowly. "I guess we can get that done."

Mom smiled at her to show her support, but I knew she was ready to throw something at the mayor.

As the girls returned to their seats, Ama saw me sitting in the back and smiled. I shot her a "thumbs-up."

During a recess in the meeting, I went out to the lobby. The girls from the environmental club were milling around, chatting about Ama's presentation.

"Hey," Ama said, when she saw me walk out of the council room.

"What's up, Ama? You guys really going to build a bird blind?" The minute I said it, I knew it was a dumb question.

"Uh-huh, we all are," she said, indicating the other girls in the group.

I bobbed my head, grinning. "Cool." I didn't know why I was grinning. "You were good in there, by the way."

"Thanks. I hope they approve. In the meantime, we're looking for volunteers, Hay." She gave me a sad-puppy look. Some of the girls giggled.

I was still grinning when people started going back into the council room.

"It looks like they're starting again," I said. "Are you staying?"

She shook her head. "We're leaving. Mom said there's nothing more for us to do tonight."

"Okay, see you in school."

"Bye." She flashed me a smile that I was still thinking about as I walked back to my seat.

The rest of the meeting was so boring I took to counting the ceiling tiles—187 by my count—and I wondered why there would be an odd number like that. I don't know how long I pondered that question, while on the microphones I dimly heard words like *abatement, easements, assessments,* but when I heard *center for cycling excellence* and *velodrome,* I paid attention. *Velodrome.* In my mind I heard Mr. Davenport on the recorder saying, *You must really want that velodrome if you're willing to part with all that money.*

The mayor was saying something about wanting to take a bunch of money out of the city's treasury to give it to some bicycle club to build a velodrome in Loveland. I remembered how Sean Baer bragged about his dad bringing a velodrome to the city as though he was hauling it around in the back of his pickup truck, but for all Sean's talk, Mr. Baer wasn't saying a word.

Mom wasn't happy. She raised her hand to be recognized to speak—that's what they all had to do, like raising your hand in class to get a hall pass. You really had to go, but you had to wait for that stupid pass, and if the teacher didn't see your raised hand, you could wait a long time.

But the mayor *did* see her hand. He looked right at her and ignored her. Mom kept her hand up and pushed it forward as though she wanted to shove it through his face, and she probably did want to do that, but he looked away.

Mr. Baer raised his hand, and the mayor immediately gave him permission to speak.

Mom was practically lying across the desk waving her hand.

Mr. Baer could not help smiling. "I move that we give a grant to the cycling club in the amount of ten thousand dollars."

"Discussion!" That was Mom shouting from the opposite end of the table.

The mayor turned his attention to her, finally. "Do you have something to say, Mrs. Smith?" He was clearly bored.

"Discussion means discussion, Mr. Mayor. I would like to talk about it before we simply give away the public's money."

Mayor Davenport sighed. "Proceed."

She gave what I thought was an intelligent speech about why it was wrong to give public money to a private club, especially when the mayor had given the council members so little information about the cycling club, but the men on council all sat there without saying a word.

"That's why I cannot support giving the club any money until we have full disclosure about them," she concluded.

"Are you finished?" the mayor asked.

"Yes."

The mayor called for a vote. When it was over the four men had voted "yes," and the three women had voted "no." The city would fork over ten thousand dollars to the cycling club.

Mom was about to blow a fuse. She and her peeps were taken by surprise, that's for sure. Sucker-punched. Her face was red, her eyes wild. I knew that I would need to be on my best behavior when we got home.

8

MOM SAID ONLY ONE WORD on the drive home: *Bastards!* She rarely swore and I knew enough to keep quiet. She slammed the car door in the garage and flung her briefcase onto the couch when we got home.

"We were set up!" I didn't know if she expected me to say something or not, so I just stood there like a dummy. "Did you see what happened? They had it all planned."

I nodded my head, wishing I could somehow sneak off to my room and close the door.

She dropped onto the couch and kicked off her shoes. She leaned her head on her hand. "They had information that we did not have. That's a violation of council ethics. They must have had a meeting of their own somewhere, probably at Paxton's," she said, referring to a bar near City Hall.

"Uh, Mom? Do you need me for anything?"

"What?" She looked up at me as if finally seeing me for the first time. "Oh, sorry, Haycorn. No, that's fine."

"Okay, then," I said, and went off to my room. I lay on my bed, thinking about the meeting. There wasn't anything I could do for her, any way that I could help her. That really pissed me off. Those guys, especially Mr. Baer and that smarmy mayor, had always rated a high smack-factor. But now, it was off the charts.

What would Dad do if he were here? I bet he would have had a talk with them after the meeting. And by "talk, I meant he would have given them a piece of his mind, until Mom hauled him back like a runaway Rottweiler. But Dad wasn't here. He was in Afghanistan. It may as well have been the moon. He didn't know anything about what Mom was going through, and it was clear I just wasn't big enough to fill in for him.

Frustrated, I tossed in bed for what seemed like hours before I finally fell asleep. Maybe I was dreaming, I don't know, but I thought I heard her crying softly. I *hoped* I was dreaming.

The next morning in home room, Ama Yendi asked me how the rest of the council meeting went. She was wearing that green T-shirt again, the one with the tree and the words *Loveland Environmental Youth Club* printed on it. I couldn't imagine she was really all that interested but she asked me anyway, so I shrugged and told her that it went alright. I was still too ticked off about it to tell her what had really happened. I'm not sure she would have understood anyway. Ama was smart, but city council stuff was complicated. If it wasn't for Mom explaining everything to me, I wouldn't have known that what had happened at the meeting was almost like stealing the people's money. I'll bet most adults didn't even know that.

"The club is going to map out the place for the bird blind today," she said, changing the subject. "We could use some help. Do you want to come?"

I looked at the big tree on the front of her shirt, noticing the way the branches curved over her body. I felt uncomfortable. I took a step back, as though standing too close to a fire.

"We're meeting at the preserve after school. Do you want to help?" She was giving me that big smile again and I knew I would do it.

"I've got soccer practice at five, so I can't stay too late but, yeah, okay. I guess I can make it."

"Cool."

Budge wasn't in my home room, so I didn't get the chance to talk to him about the bird blind thing until we were on the bus heading home.

"And you're going?"

"I guess."

"Sounds lame."

"Why?"

"It just does. A bird blind? No one even knows what that is."

"Some people do." I don't know why I was defending the project, it had nothing to do with me, but I saw Ama's face in my mind and thought I should. "Why don't you come with me?"

We were passing the post office. Fat Mister Nightingale waddled toward the door. He was carrying a bunch of mail wrapped with a rubber band.

"I can't go even if I wanted to. Merv would kill me."

"Why?"

"It's work. He wouldn't let me." He patted his chest. "My heart."

Sometimes I wondered if Budge wasn't just dogging it with that heart thing. I mean, it got him excused from running laps in gym—and most of the gym classes for that matter—he didn't mow the lawn, didn't shovel snow. His sisters did all that stuff. But he loved to watch basketball on TV, and he would shoot hoops in my driveway. And I knew once in a while he would sneak a cigarette from his dad's pack. His heart condition seemed really convenient at times. Must be nice. I wouldn't mind being sick like that.

"Anyway, I have to go to the doctor today."

"For real?" He nodded. "Okay." He was often going to the doctor for check-ups and stuff. That was the one thing that made me think he really might not be faking it.

When I got home, I checked the mailbox, hoping there might be a letter from Dad, but it was all junk. I dropped my bag in my bedroom, got on my bike, and rode out to the East Loveland Nature Preserve. It wasn't far away and mostly downhill. An easy ride.

Three soccer mom cars, readily identifiable by soccer ball decals in their windows, were parked in the VFW parking lot next to the preserve. I left my bike near one of them and walked down the path into the woods.

Here it was, September heading for October, and the trees were all yellow and dried up looking. Many of them were already losing their leaves. Dead leaves crunched under my feet as I walked the path. The white trunks of some huge sycamores along the creek gleamed in the sun; I read somewhere that the Shawnee Indians called them "ghost trees."

The preserve had been the brainy idea of some people who thought the city already had enough soccer and baseball fields and should preserve more green space. Mom liked the idea. She helped the group get the city's approval to build the preserve. The men on the council weren't happy about the idea. They wanted to build condos there, until they learned the creek often flooded over the property. Then they were only too happy to get rid of it and make it a nature preserve.

A lot of volunteers, including some school groups, worked on building trails through the preserve, throwing down mulch on the paths they cut to keep them clear of weeds. Someone made tree identification signs and put them up along the trails. Someone else stuck a bluebird house in a meadow.

I walked along the trail until I saw the girls and a few adults ahead. There were a couple guys I knew as well, including Sean Baer. I couldn't believe it. I was about to turn around and leave when Ama spotted me and waved. I was stuck.

Everybody was standing around in a little clearing beside the trail. There wasn't a whole lot of work going on as far as I could tell. One of the adults held a bunch of wooden stakes with red ribbons nailed to them. Two girls were on their knees in the grass, stretching a measuring tape between them.

"Haycorn," Ama said, walking over to me. "Do you know how to make a bird blind?"

"No."

"You pull his hat down over his eyes."

"Jeezul, Ama," I said, but I couldn't help laughing.

"Haycorn Smith!" Sean called out, by way of greeting. He waved to me. I would have ignored him completely if Ama hadn't been standing there, but I didn't want her to think I was a jerk, so I gave him a half-hearted wave in return.

"Is Sean helping, too?" I said.

She gave me a shrug that could mean *yes* or *no*, I didn't know which, but she said, "I'm glad you came." She smiled at me, and I swear, that smile socked me right in the chest. She could sock me in the chest like that all day long. She swept her arm over the clearing. "We're measuring out the space now. We want to put some feeding stations in the meadow and put the blind right near the path. That way people could go inside and watch the birds through the windows."

"Sounds good." I didn't really care a whole lot about the bird blind, but Ama did, and the excitement in her voice was catching.

"We'd really like to get it up before the winter. That's not much time, so we'll need a lot of help."

She stood close, looking at me. Her eyes were so dark. Before I had time to think I heard myself say, "I can help."

She grabbed my arm. "Oh, Haycorn, that would be wonderful!"

An hour later, after the mapping out was all finished and I was riding my bike home, the place where she had held my arm still warmed me like sunburn.

9

W E GOT A FEW EMAILS from Dad. Mom was always in a
good mood after getting them, and I was happy, too. They
never said much—it was hot, he was busy but okay, he missed us,
that kind of thing—and the reason why was that he was not
allowed to give us too much information. The Army support
groups asked families not to tell their soldiers too much personal
stuff that might be bad for their morale. So, the emails weren't
great, but they were better than nothing.

I had a lot of stuff going on. There was soccer, the ghost voice—
which Budge and I really needed to check out, despite what Mom had
said—the thing about the money, although Mom would probably
have to figure that out, and then, of course, building the bird blind.

I decided to tackle the castle ghost, even though I knew if Mom
found out she would ground me for the next one hundred years.
Budge and me were really on to something. We could become
famous if we could prove ghosts were real. We would have to take

the risk. What if Columbus's mother had told him he couldn't sail because he might fall off the edge of the world? Where would we be today? No, I had to become Paranormal Columbus!

I text-messaged Budge and soon, we were in my bedroom, figuring out the best way to investigate the castle for ghosts.

Budge took inventory of what equipment we had, which was not much. "I wish we had some of the gear they use on TV."

"That would be cool, but we don't."

"We could make some dowsing rods like the TV ghosthunters use."

"Dowsing rods? Have you ever used them?" Budge said he hadn't. "I once saw a guy from the cable company use them. He was working next door and he had one in each hand and was slowly walking back and forth across the lawn. When the rods crossed over each other, he would spray a spot of red paint on the grass. When he was done, the other guys dug up where he painted the spots, and they found the cable running under the ground there."

"That's awesome," Budge said. "How do we make them?"

"A guy on TV made them out of coat hangers. All we need is a pair of wire cutters."

I went to my closet and took out four hangers. Then I went to Dad's toolbox in the garage, got a pair of wire cutters and brought them back to my room. I untwisted the hangers so that we had four pieces of wire, more or less straight. With the wire cutters, I cut off two pieces of straight wire, then bent one end of each so that I wound up with a pair of L-shaped wires. Budge picked them up, holding the shorter ends in his hands, the longer ends pointing forward like guns.

"Bang! Bang! You're dead," he said. "Oh, wait, you're a ghost, you're already dead."

"Great. Do you think they'll work?"

"We'll find out," he said. He made another pair of rods from the wire. We were set.

The next day after school we rode to the castle. We had Budge's camcorder and Mom's digital voice recorder since she still held onto

Budge's. And we had the dowsing rods. It was a weekday and a light drizzle was in the air, so there was no one else at the castle. Perfect.

People who didn't know better might wonder what we were doing at the castle in broad daylight, trying to find ghosts, when all the TV shows featured ghosthunters working overnight, stumbling around in the dark, scaring themselves with their own shadows. What I learned from all my reading about ghosts was that they were present twenty-four-seven. They weren't like bats that only came out at night. Ghost hunting at night was sometimes better than doing it in the daytime because everything was usually quieter and the darkness sometimes made it easier for apparitions to show up on video. Plus, it was scarier in the dark. Other than that, it didn't really make much difference when you chased spirits.

We stood in the shelter of the main gate, listening to the soft patter of the rain in the trees. Yellow leaves were falling. We heard a woodpecker knock loudly on a tree somewhere along the river. The castle stood behind us, gloomy and dark with rain.

"What do you want to try first?" Budge asked.

"Let me have the voice recorder." He handed it to me and I turned it on, tucking it into the pocket of my denim shirt. "You're supposed to record everything," I said. "Okay, how about we try some dowsing?"

"Sounds good, dude."

I held a pair of dowsing rods in my hands and started slowly walking across the yard toward the stables. "Budge and me at the stables, Loveland Castle," I said, for the benefit of the recorder. You're supposed to always say where you are and who is with you. I held the rods out while he aimed the camcorder at me. I didn't feel anything weird as I held the rods, although I didn't know what I was supposed to feel. Vibrations, maybe? We ducked into the stables to get out of the rain.

"Budge and Haycorn inside the stables," I said.

Budge held the camera steady and slowly panned around the stables. He lowered the camera. "What now? This is where you heard that laugh, right?" I nodded. "Hear anything now?"

We stood silently for a few minutes. A slow trickle of water echoed from somewhere outside, but other than that, it was quiet. "No, nothing."

"Whoa!" Budge suddenly took a quick step closer to me, "What the heck was that?"

"What was what?"

"Dude, it felt like somebody touched me on the arm!" He was rubbing his elbow. "You didn't feel anything?"

"No. Are you trying to scare me?"

"It was creepy, dude! It felt cold." He was looking around the room, trying to see whatever was there, but of course, we were alone.

I'll admit it, seeing how freaked out Budge was gave me a chill and freaked me out a little. But I was excited, too. "Awesome!" I whispered. "Let's try the rods again." I held out the rods as though I was holding a pair of pistols. In a louder voice I said, "Is there anyone here that would like to talk to us?"

We waited in silence, Budge glancing around the room nervously. I could feel my heart thumping.

"We won't hurt you," I said, imitating the words the TV ghosthunters used, although I could never figure out how you could hurt a ghost since it was already dead. Nothing happened. The rods in my hands continued to point forward.

"We … we just want to know about you," Budge chimed in, his voice shaky.

"If you're here, would you please let us know? Can you make the rods in my hands move to show us that you are here?" I waited a few moments and was about to speak again when a slight vibration tingled my right hand. It grew stronger. I had the urge to drop the rods and run, but somehow, I stayed put. The rod was starting to turn to the left. "Budge!"

He raised the camcorder and focused on the dowsing rods. "Holy cow! They're moving!"

"Is that you?" My voice trembled. "Are … you making the rods … move? See if you can make them cross."

They were both moving now, slowly, but steadily. I kept my hands as still as possible, trying hard not to move them myself.

I glanced at Budge and saw the camera shaking in his hand. "Budge, keep the camera steady!"

"I'm trying, dude! I'm trying," Budge said.

Gradually, the right rod turned left, and the left rod turned right until they finally formed an "X." A shiver rippled my spine.

"Jeezul-Pete! Are you getting this?" I said.

"Oh, yeah. Incredible!"

"Rods have crossed!" I said for the recorder.

Amazing! It was just like on TV. We had contacted a ghost and it was talking to us through the dowsing rods. But even the TV ghosthunters didn't know exactly how ghosts could do that; something to do with ghosts being creatures of energy and being able to use that energy to talk with us.

I stood there, breathing hard, looking at the rods the ghost had crossed at my request. It wanted to talk with us. "Thank you," I said. I dropped one rod on the ground and held the other in my right hand, this time with the long end pointing down as if I held a gun and was going to shoot myself in the foot.

"We'd really like to know more about you and hope you will continue to talk to us. I'm going to ask you some questions. You can answer *yes* by making the rod in my hand swing. If the answer is *no*, you don't have to do anything at all. Okay?" I swallowed hard. "Here we go."

We should have been prepared but we hadn't bothered to think about any questions for the ghost beforehand, so we were winging it all the way.

"Are you a man or a woman?" Budge asked.

I shot him a look. "He can't answer that with *yes* or *no*."

"Oh yeah, right. Are you a woman?" The rod in my hand remained still. "Are you a man?" he asked.

"Jeezul, if he's not a woman, he's got to be a man! What's wrong with you, Budge?"

"Whatever," Budge said, irritated, but he kept the camera rolling.

I took a deep breath. "Did you die here?" I thought I may as well get to the point.

The rod in my hand shook and then gently rocked from side to side a few seconds before stopping. *Yes.*

"Oh, my god! Thank you."

"If he died here, he must be the guy that built this place," Budge said. "Didn't you say he burnt himself up here?"

"Yes, but he actually died in the hospital. There could have been someone else that died on this spot, maybe a long time ago before the castle was even built. They say ghosts haunt a location no matter what buildings may be on it, so the ghost could be anyone."

"Maybe someone eaten by wolves, like a hundred years ago or something?" Budge asked. Before I could answer, Budge said, "Hey, ghost, were you eaten by wolves?"

No response. "Jeezul, Budge!"

He shrugged. "Okay, let's ask him his name."

Sometimes Budge's simple ideas are right on. The problem was that I was a little worked up and could not remember the man's name, the guy that built the castle, so we just started throwing out as many male names as we could think of, all without a response from the rod. Then, just after Budge had asked the ghost if his name was Ezekiel—I had no idea how he came up with that one—the castle builder's name came to me: *Harry.* Sure enough, when I asked the ghost if Harry was his name, that rod began to swing back and forth as though the ghost was ringing a bell.

We stared at each other.

"Holy crap!" Budge said.

"You can say that again."

"Holy crap!"

The air around us suddenly turned so cold, our breath condensed into puffy little clouds. Budge's teeth chattered. I didn't know if he was scared, cold, or both. I know I was. Both. I don't know how long it was before we snapped out of it and went back to work, but by that time the rod was hanging loosely in my hand and the frigid air had disappeared as quickly as it had formed.

"Are you still here, Harry?" I asked.

Nothing.

"Harry, can you talk to us?"

There was no reply. The stable now felt oddly calm and peaceful.

Budge was still rubbing the chill from his arms. "I think he's gone."

"Yes, I think so." I stuck the dowsing rods in my belt. "How awesome was that?"

He grinned. "It was pretty sweet, alright."

We were still pumped when we got back to Budge's house. We already had the EVP—Harry's voice on the recorder—from the last time and now we had the video of the moving dowsing rods. We were building a strong case for the haunted castle.

We sat on the floor in Budge's bedroom, the door securely closed against his nosey sisters.

I took Mom's recorder out of my pocket. "Let's give a listen," I said, turning it on.

As expected, we heard our voices and it was exciting to relive our encounter with Harry's ghost, but what really got our attention, what made the hairs on the back of my neck stand up, I swear, was when we heard a raspy man's voice whisper, *the wall.*

"Whoa," Budge said, his eyes wide.

"You can say that again," I said, but I quickly held up my hand. "No, don't."

"What do you think that means?" Budge said.

I shook my head. "No idea. Let's play it again. Maybe we didn't hear it right."

We must have replayed it a million times but, no, *the wall* was what we heard.

10

OUR EVIDENCE TOLD US TWO THINGS. First, the castle was haunted. Nothing anyone could say would change our minds about that. And second, the ghost was trying to help us catch the mayor! We had to act. I'd clue Mom into what we knew but I decided that, no matter what she thought, Budge and I would not back off.

"I think we should tell my mom about all the stuff we got from the castle. The evidence." We were sitting in the school cafeteria. Noisy as usual, and no one else sat at our table, so I thought it was okay to tell him what I had been thinking about all morning in class.

"You think so?" Budge said, picking the pepperoni off his pizza.

"Why do you do that?"

He looked up. "Do what?"

"That." I pointed to the neat little stack of pepperoni slices on his plate.

"I don't like pepperoni."

"Then get the plain pizza instead."

"But, dude, everyone says the pepperoni kind is better."

"You're a piece of work," I said, taking his pepperoni and popping it in my mouth. "I think my mom should see what we've got."

"Why?"

"There's got to be some connection between our evidence and what we saw go down that night with those two guys, don't you think? And if one of them really was the mayor …"

"Your mom wouldn't tell my dad about our ghost hunt, would she?"

"Not if I ask her not to."

"Okay, I'm good with that."

I was going to say more but just then Mike Kreutzer plopped his lunch tray down on our table. Sean wasn't with him, for once, so I didn't mind him sitting with us. "What's up, men?" he said.

Before we could answer, Mike said, "Hey, check it out." He pointed with his chin to a nearby table where Ama Yendi and some of her girlfriends were sitting. Sean stood by her chair, talking with her, his lunch tray in his hands. Mike grinned. "Sean's squeeze." He wiggled his eyebrows.

"What?" I said.

"Ama and Sean."

Budge's hand froze halfway to his mouth as he looked at me.

"You've got to be kidding me," I said.

Mike shook his head. "No, man, that's what Sean says. He said he touched her boob once."

"Holy crap!" Budge muttered.

My food sat on my tray untouched. I looked at Sean and Ama and wanted to punch Sean in the face. He was lying, he must have been. She would never let him do that. But I wanted to punch Mike's face in, too, for saying such a freaking thing in the first place. Instead, I kept my hands under the table and sat there, my anger filling me up like an empty bottle.

Budge leaned across the table. "Haycorn?"

I glared at Sean, who was finally walking away from Ama's table.

"Haycorn, are you okay?" Budge said.

"Sean says she's hot," Mike said.

That was it. I jumped up from the table, grabbed my tray and stomped off. Budge didn't follow me and as I left, I heard Mike say, "What's his problem?"

I stormed into homeroom and dropped into my seat. The room was empty; everyone else was still at lunch. I felt like I was going to explode. What could she possibly see in that little creep? *Jeezul!* The guy was such a turd, how could any girl want to be his girlfriend? I was angry with Sean, but also angry with Ama. I felt as though she had cheated on me, even though we were not boyfriend and girlfriend. I mean, not really. But what was wrong with me? Wasn't I as good as Sean?

I hardly noticed when Budge sat beside me.

"You alright, man?" When I didn't answer, he said, "Don't listen to Mike. He doesn't know what he's talking about."

"Oh, no?"

"No. She's too good for Sean. You know that. They could never be an item."

That's what I would have thought, too, only Sean was there the day the girls were working on the bird blind and now, here he was, chatting her up in the cafeteria. It didn't seem to me that Ama thought Sean was beneath her. I think she liked the attention. She smiled at him; what was *that* all about?

"You know Sean is full of horsedooky. You can't believe anything he says."

"You were there, Budge. Didn't you see them?"

"She was just being nice."

"Oh, sure."

"Come on, dude." Just then, some of the other kids started returning to the room. "Got to go, Hay. Be cool." He got up to return to his own homeroom.

Ama walked into the room, talking with Evie Parker, one of her friends. She laughed about something—probably me—and never even looked in my direction as she took her seat. My ears felt like they were burning. I didn't want to look at her, but I couldn't help myself. She sat at her desk, straightening her books, pretending that nothing had happened. *Yeah, right.*

Ama wasn't in my next two classes, which I hardly paid attention to, and then I was on the bus. She rode a different bus home—the same one as Sean, it suddenly dawned on me. That was just great. Budge sat next to me as usual and tried to get me to talk, or to laugh, but I wasn't having any of it.

STILL P.O.d? my cell phone asked later that night. Budge.

Y.

STOP, he said. GOT WRK 2 DO.

?

HARRY.

It wasn't exactly that I had forgotten about the ghost and the evidence we had collected at the castle, or that we had said we were going to clue Mom in, but with the Ama and Sean drama, I lost focus. Budge was right, though, we needed to figure out what was going on at the castle. I couldn't let some girl get in the way of that. No professional ghosthunter would act that way. I sighed. *Deal with all that stuff later*, I told myself.

K, I typed, UR RIT.

PLAY HARRY 4 HR.

I knew he meant that I should play the recorder for Mom. *K*, I said, FBM.

P911, Budge answered, G2R.

I sat on my bed, thinking about the best way to tell Mom. Usually, straight up with her was the way to go. She had already heard the voice the first time, anyway, so this latest recording shouldn't be much of a shock. Or, so I hoped. I picked up the recorder and walked out to the study.

She was looking at some kind of graph on her computer. Red, green, and blue lines, but I had no idea what they were all about. I didn't understand a whole lot about her job as an environmental technician. It was complicated, that much I knew, and you had to be pretty good at science, which she was. A large aluminum case lay open on the floor beside her chair. Some electronic stuff nestled in a black foam insert within the case.

"Hi, Mom. What are you doing?"

"Hi, Sweetie." She swiveled in her chair to face me.

Sweetie. That was positive; she was in a good mood.

"I'm just doing some research for the department, and I need to do an equipment check for tomorrow," she said, pointing at the case.

"What's tomorrow?"

"We're checking out one of the police stations."

I squatted to get a closer look at the electronic gear in the case. "What is all this stuff?"

"Mostly EMF meters."

"Hey, the ghosthunters on TV use those things!"

She laughed. "Really? We use them all the time in the health department, but I don't think we have any ghosts running around there." She picked one up from the case and showed it to me. It was a little metal box with a display window and when she turned it on some green numbers appeared in the box. "Do you know what these are used for?"

"Kind of."

"EMF stands for electromagnetic frequency. Anything electrical—the TV, computer, toaster, power lines—gives off electromagnetic radiation."

"Is that a bad thing?"

"Well, that's what people like me study. Some people think that too much electromagnetic radiation can cause health problems, but we don't really know for sure yet. These meters measure the frequency of electromagnetic radiation being given off by appliances, wires, a lot of other things." She held the EMF meter closer to the computer and the numbers in the box went higher. When she moved it away, the numbers dropped. "It's simple to use. Want to try it?"

She handed me the meter. I walked around the room, holding it by light switches, a radio, any electrical thing I could find.

"Tell me what ghosthunters do with them," Mom said, as I continued to test it out.

"Pretty much what I'm doing now. They walk around with them, hoping to get some high numbers."

"Then what?"

"If they get those numbers and there wasn't anything electrical around, then they think a ghost is present," I said.

"Do they think ghosts give off electromagnetic radiation?"

"Yes."

"Can they prove that?" she asked.

I shrugged. "Who knows?" I handed the meter to her. I sat on the ottoman near the desk. She put it back in the case. "Mom, do you remember that strange voice on Budge's recorder?"

"Your ghost?" She smiled.

"Yes." I placed the recorder we had used the last time at the castle on the desk. "Listen to this."

I turned on the recorder. She arched an eyebrow and looked at me as she heard me and Budge talking excitedly while the dowsing rods did their thing.

"I'll explain all that later, just keep listening."

And then, there it was, that gravelly voice speaking to us. Harry, the ghost.

Mom studied the recorder, as though she could see right through it. "Play it again."

I played it back several times, Mom turning her ear to the recorder, listening intently. Finally, she sat back in her chair, her eyes still trained on the recorder.

"Well?"

"It certainly sounds like a man's voice," she said. "It sounds like the other voice."

I nodded. "Yes, it's the same."

"Are you sure there was no one else there besides you and Budge?"

"No one, Mom."

"Well," she said.

She was thinking about what she had heard.

"What did it sound like to you, Mom? What did you hear the ghost say?"

"The ghost? What I heard was a man's voice—an old man, maybe—speaking. It wasn't clear to me right away. At first, I thought he said something about a mall, but after a while I recognized he was saying, *the wall*."

"Exactly!" I nearly fell off the ottoman. "That's what Budge and me heard, too." This was awesome. Now we had an adult, a member of city council, too, saying she heard the same thing we had heard. We weren't just two crazy kids.

"But Haycorn, what did he mean by that?"

"That's the million-dollar question." A question for which I had no answer. At least, not yet.

11

M OM CALLED MY CELL to tell me she would be late coming
home from work. I told her not to worry, I would make
dinner.

"Really?"

She didn't sound too confident in my cooking abilities, but I
could cook eggs, hot dogs, and some other stuff.

"Sure, no sweat. Dad would do it for you if he was here."

"You're right, Sweetie, he would. Okay, go ahead. See you soon."

She thanked me for dinner but didn't say a whole lot more
when we sat down to eat the Fritos pie I made, even though I
added some baby carrots from a bag as a side; Mom was Mrs.
Health and was big on veggies.

It had become our habit to switch on the nightly news as we
ate dinner—a practice we had started only after Dad's deployment
to Afghanistan—and that's what we were watching now. CNN, I
think it was.

There was some news about the troops getting ready to come home from Iraq, even though there were still car bombings almost every day, it seemed. I wished Dad had been sent to Iraq instead of Afghanistan. He might already be on his way home if that had happened. But no, he was in a place that seemed to be getting more and more dangerous.

Mom slowly worked on her Fritos pie, her eyes fixed on the TV.

"Don't let it get cold, Mom. It's best when it's still warm."

She smiled at me. "I'm fine, Hay, thanks."

I began to think she didn't really like Fritos pie.

A news story from Afghanistan came on. Some general was talking about how the Taliban was getting stronger in one of the provinces and I wondered if that was where Dad was located. We had no idea where he was, or what he was doing.

Then a reporter wearing a helmet and body armor came on. The ticker below his picture said he was in Helmand Province, but the scenery behind him looked like every other picture I had seen from Afghanistan. Beige and dusty. The ground was beige and dusty. The buildings were beige and dusty. Even the people looked beige and dusty. Only the sky was a different color, a bright blue. The reporter said an Afghan soldier working with American soldiers had suddenly turned on the Americans and shot three of them dead before someone blew him away.

"Jeezul-Pete!"

Mom didn't say anything. She just sat there looking at the screen. Her Fritos pie was getting cold.

So much for friends, I thought. Why would he do such a thing? Didn't he know our guys were there to help his country? I wondered what Dad would do if the soldier next to him—a guy he was supposed to trust—pointed his rifle at him. Would Dad shoot him? Would he be able to protect himself? It made my stomach queasy just thinking about it.

"I don't get it, Mom." She gave me a look that said she didn't get it either.

Now, a couple beige Hummers were driving down a beige road, throwing up big clouds of beige dust and then, a commercial, a little green lizard selling car insurance.

"Mom, is Dad safe?" It was a stupid question, I know. How could she answer it? But something inside me hoped maybe she could.

"Oh, Sweetie." She hugged me. "I hope so. Let's pray that he is."

And I did. We weren't big churchgoers. We went now and then, but that night I prayed to God to keep Dad safe. He had been away for over a month, but I had never prayed to God for anything. I didn't see the point. I mean, two football teams pray before their game for a win, but only one wins. So, did that mean God was angry with one of the teams? But still, with Dad in a dangerous place, I figured it couldn't hurt to pray. Maybe it was the news that hit me so hard, but for the first time since he had been gone, I felt tightness in my chest— a weight as though someone was sitting on me—and I worried about him. I knew Dad would say not to worry, he was fine, but I couldn't help myself. So, I prayed, and I guess I cried a little too.

I had a hard time falling asleep, and when I finally did, bad dreams kept waking me. I couldn't remember any of them in detail. All I could remember was darkness full of shadowy figures and sound and fury. As a result, I was in a lousy mood the next morning when I headed out for the school bus. Budge was already at the stop, sitting on the curb. He was eating a Slim-Jim.

"How can you eat that stuff so early in the morning?"

"Good morning to you, too, Hay." I sat on the curb beside him. "You look like crap," he said.

"Thanks, I love you, too. Had a rough night last night, couldn't sleep."

"Thinking about Ama." He smirked, as though he knew everything.

"Wrong, idiot. I was thinking about my dad." He nodded but didn't say anything. "I wish he was home."

"Yeah," Budge said, just as the school bus was grinding up our street.

We got on and sat down but didn't say much. At the next stop, Evie Parker, Ama's friend, got on. She was a cute blonde and she gave us a little smile as she passed our seat, but I was having none of it. I didn't want to give her anything she and Ama could use to make me look like a fool. Budge, on the other hand, flashed her a big smile in return.

"Oh, my god! You and Evie?" I felt like that American soldier must have felt when he found himself facing his Afghan so-called friend.

He shrugged his shoulders. "She's cute."

"You *like* her. Does she know?"

"No."

Jeezul. That's all I needed now, to have Evie and Ama turn Budge against me too. Who would I have left?

I was in a funk throughout the day but late that night, just after I finished playing Minecraft on my computer—my avatar's name was Juan Cuervo—an email came in from Dad.

It read:

Hey, Buddy,

I've got a little down-time, so I thought I'd write you. I hope you and your mom are doing fine. I'm okay—tired, working long, mostly boring hours, but okay. I miss you, Hay, you and your mom and I can't wait until this job is done and I'm home again. You know, I was thinking that it's been a long time since you and I canoed the river. We'll definitely do that as soon as I'm back. I know you're helping out as best you can at home, son, and I'm proud of you for doing that. I'm sure it's not easy, but I'm counting on you to be a man and to help your mom in any way you can. I know you can do it, Hay. Until the next time,

Love,
Dad

I sat there reading over the email several times, and then brushed away the tears I didn't know had formed in my eyes. I ran to Mom's bedroom and knocked on the door. She was smiling like it was Christmas morning when she opened it.

"Let me guess. You got an email from Dad."

"Yes!"

"I did, too, Sweetie."

"Do you want to hear what he said?"

She looked thoughtful and then said, "No, Hay, I don't think I do. Dad wanted to send you a private message and I think we should keep it that way. Is that alright with you?"

I nodded.

"Okay." She kissed me on top of my head. "Goodnight, Haycorn." She closed her door.

I went back to my room and lay on my bed, looking up at the Lionel Messi poster. "So, what do you think of that, Lionel?" He didn't reply.

I rolled onto my side and closed my eyes. Whatever had been eating away at me all day long was gone. No more worries about Ama or Sean, no thoughts about the ghost or the fishy business at the castle. Nothing. All I thought about was me and Dad quietly paddling a canoe down the Little Miami, the bright white sycamore trees glowing along the river, their big yellow leaves floating in the air like angels, while a great blue heron stood in the shallows. The canoe skimmed along the water, and I could feel the river flowing beneath me as I let it carry me away to sleep.

12

THERE WAS ANOTHER city council meeting the next evening and I went with Mom. If she was still investigating whatever had gone down with the two guys at the castle, I thought I should go with her to the meetings. She might need my protection.

Budge was less than excited. I'm sure he regretted allowing me to talk him into coming with us, but there was no way out now.

The mayor called the meeting to order, and the public forum began.

"How does your mom stay awake?" Budge whispered.

I looked up at her and she was not only awake, but obviously paying close attention to each of the speakers, unlike Mayor Davenport, who was reading the newspaper, as usual.

After the forum, a guy named Walter Ambrose made a special presentation to the council about the proposed velodrome. When he came to the podium at the front of the room, we got a good view of him.

"Budge!" My stomach churned. "Check it out. Isn't that the guy we saw at the castle that night?"

"The guy in the car?"

"Yes."

We studied the guy. Tall, balding, with a moustache.

"Could be, but it was dark, and we only saw him for a second. I'm not sure."

It turned out Mr. Ambrose was the developer who wanted to build the velodrome in Loveland. A lot of people thought the velodrome was a stupid idea and a waste of money. But as I listened to him, he talked as though everything was a go. He made it sound like he could have bulldozers in town tomorrow.

I watched Mom. She was listening intently, a serious expression on her face. I didn't think she was buying what the developer was selling.

"That's got to be the guy," I said to Budge.

It was always hard for me to tell what got done at city council meetings. Sometimes they were only talking about things, other times they were voting and putting things into action. I thought Mr. Ambrose was just giving the council a report on what he hoped to do, but that nothing was going to happen for some time yet.

As the three of us drove home, I said, "Mom? That Ambrose guy?"

"Walter Ambrose."

"He's got two first names?" I asked.

She laughed. "Yes, what about him?"

"Budge and me think he's the guy we recorded talking to the mayor at the castle."

I thought she would slam on the brakes, completely stunned, but she kept driving calmly, her eyes fixed on the road ahead.

"I had that same suspicion myself. I've heard him speak before and I recognized the voice on the recorder. Does he look like the man you saw that night?"

"Kind of. It was pretty dark."

She turned onto Glen Lake Road. "You boys had a camcorder with you, right? Did you happen to get any video of the men?"

"We were too scared, Mrs. Smith," Budge said, from the back seat. "We forgot all about it."

She nodded. "That's understandable. But you two did see the man and you both think it might be Mr. Ambrose?"

"Yes," we said, simultaneously.

She pulled into the driveway of Budge's house.

"Later, dude," he said, as he got out of the car.

"See you."

"Listen, Hay," Mom said, when we got home a few minutes later, "I don't want you and Budge talking to anyone about this, is that clear?"

"We won't." I dropped onto the sofa. "But there's something wrong about what we saw, isn't there?"

She sat beside me. "Remember, this is just between us but, yes, I think there is something wrong. I can't think of any logical reason why the mayor would be at the castle in the middle of the night meeting with Ambrose. They talked about money on the recording, but you two didn't see any money, right?"

"Right, but we did see the mayor carrying a briefcase. I bet it was full of money."

"I don't know how to prove that. It could be Ambrose paid off the mayor in order to get his approvals through so he could build his velodrome, but I don't know how to prove that, either."

"But you've got the recording and me and Budge are witnesses."

"The recording sounds suspicious, that's for sure, and maybe a good lawyer could make the case for us, but I'd really like to have stronger evidence." She frowned at me. "As for you two as witnesses, I think you might not be taken seriously."

"Because we're kids?"

She nodded. "Exactly. A lawyer for the other side could say kids are easily influenced by their imaginations, that they lie ..."

"We're not lying!"

She patted my knee. "I know you're not, but a sharp lawyer would say that in court. He could make you two sound completely unreliable."

"That stinks."

"Yes, it does, Hay, but that's the way it is."

We sat quietly on the couch. I was thinking how things might be different if Dad was here. Maybe he would know what to do right now because I sure didn't. How could I help Mom? Being a kid sucked, but there must be *something* I could do.

"Hay, tell me again exactly what you boys saw that night. Don't leave anything out."

When I finished telling her everything all over again, she said, "Okay, so you saw the man you think was Ambrose hand over a case to the mayor."

"Yes."

"And then Ambrose drove away, leaving the mayor holding the case."

"Yes."

"You said the mayor then went inside the castle, remained there for a few minutes, and then came out again. But he didn't have the case with him."

"That's right. So, that means…"

"The case might still be in the castle."

"Jeezul!"

"Of course, it's been a while since you two were there. It might not be there anymore. Maybe the mayor came back for it later."

"Mom, we've got to go check it out!"

"Absolutely not! I don't want you or Budge anywhere near the castle now. If we're right, then the castle could be a dangerous place. We don't know if the mayor has picked up the case yet and the last thing I want is for you two to be there when he returns for it."

"Aww, come on, Mom! We can go there right now and look for it. What are the chances the mayor would be there at the same time?"

"No, Haycorn! I mean it. The castle is off limits for you two."

That did not make me happy. It seemed like an easy thing to drive to the castle and look around. I was sure the mayor wasn't hanging around the castle twenty-four-seven, waiting for an all-clear before snatching the case. In fact, he probably already had it. But Mom was serious about this, I could see that. I needed another angle.

"Why don't you call the cops and have them come with us? You're a city council person, they'll listen to you."

"No. We can't involve the police just yet. Until I have more evidence, I can't let anyone know what we suspect. It's on the record if we call in the police, and the mayor would know about it immediately."

"Then what do we do?"

"I don't know, Hay. I've got to think."

That didn't sound like much of a solution to me.

She went off into the study and I sat on the couch, texting Budge.

HEY HAY, Budge wrote, SUP?

U TLK 2 ANY1 ABT CASL?

NO Y?

GUD DONT, I wrote, CLD B TRBL

?

TEL U MOR 2MOR.

GR8 GUD BY ME, Budge said.z

K CU.

GN.

It wasn't much of a talk, I know, but I wanted to make sure Budge got the word to keep his mouth shut. I could count on him to keep our secrets—usually—but if he had the hots for Evie Parker, which I was pretty sure he did, and he was hoping to impress her, it didn't hurt to remind him again. Who knows what he could tell her?

The next day at school I told him what Mom had said about the castle being an unsafe place. "This needs to be kept secret, Budge."

He narrowed his eyes and nodded. "Got it. This is top secret stuff, like in a spy movie."

"Yeah, whatever, just don't talk about the castle to anyone." Just then I caught sight of Evie Parker walking in the hall. "And I mean *anyone*. Get it?"

He nodded. "Sure, Hay, but what do we do now? Should we go and try to find the case?"

"Jeezul, Budge! Did you hear anything I just said? No, we don't look for the case ..." I stopped short because Evie and a couple other kids were close by, but I shot him a warning look to just keep his big mouth zipped.

He was looking at Evie now and I hoped her smile hadn't fried his brain so much that he would forget about our secret. I had never seen him like this before and it had me worried. I was beginning to think I didn't know Budge as well as I thought I did. Everything would fall apart if he blabbed to Evie. That worried me. Then, I saw Ama coming out of a classroom and I felt a jolt. Was I just jealous of Budge and Evie?

13

I TURNED AWAY and busied myself with my locker. I had the door open so I could pretend I didn't see Evie. It didn't work.

"Hey, Corn," she said.

Ho, ho, ho, good one, Evie. With Budge standing beside her and Mike and Sean right behind him, I was trapped. "Hey," I mumbled, my back to her.

"Are you going to help us this weekend?"

I grabbed a book from out of the locker and slammed the door shut. I sighed and turned to Evie. "What are you talking about?"

She smiled. "The bird blind. We're going to start working on it this weekend."

"You're part of that?" Budge asked.

Evie said she was, and I could see the wheels spinning in Budge's brain. They were rusty wheels but spinning all the same. Something told me Mister-who-cares-about-the-bird-blind might be changing his mind. With all the other stuff I was dealing with, I know I didn't have time to take on a construction project.

"Mike and me will be there," Sean said. Mike nodded in agreement.

"And I should care, why?"

They looked at each other, confused.

"We're just saying, Hay," Mike said, sticking his hands into his pockets.

"Ama wanted to know if you'd be coming," said Evie.

"Really."

"Yes." Evie studied my face. "What's with you, Haycorn?"

"Why does she want me to come? Does she need a good laugh?"

Evie's smile disappeared. "I don't get it. What do you mean?"

I turned back to the locker and angrily spun the lock. "Never mind. Forget it."

"Whatever." Evie walked off, Mike and Sean trailing behind.

"What's your problem, dude?" Budge said. He was angry. "You were a complete jerk with Evie. She didn't do anything to you."

I turned to face him. "Don't worry about it." I started walking down the hall.

He was close beside me, too close. "What's that supposed to mean? Why are you acting this way?"

I shot him a sidelong glance. "Back off, Budge."

His face got red, and his lips tightened. He was walking so close to me that he bumped against my shoulder, maybe on purpose. "Back off?"

This conversation, if it was a conversation, was going downhill quickly. I knew if anybody should back off it was probably me. And yet, I didn't stop. It was like sledding in the woods. There are a million trees standing there on the hillside and you know at the speed you're going, it's a safe bet you're going to slam into one of them, but you push yourself down the slope anyway.

"Mind your own business, Budge."

He stopped and gave me a hard look. I kept walking.

"Screw you, Haycorn," he said, to my back.

I left him standing there in the hall. I could almost feel the heat coming from him.

Budge's mother picked him up from school—another doctor's appointment—so he wasn't on the bus home with me. That was a good thing. I was still angry, although I didn't know what I was angry about, but I was also embarrassed. He was my best friend. We fought when we were little but now, hardly ever. I'm sure he thought I was a jerk.

I stared out the window, seeing everything and nothing at the same time. The bus came up the hill and drove past the painted canoe on display by the gazebo—one of several canoes that had been painted by different artists and placed throughout the town—and I thought of Dad again. I remembered that Saturday morning at the garage when I had been grounded. It seemed like years ago instead of days. I remembered asking him if he would go if his unit was deployed—a dumb question—and his answer that it was his duty to go. I was proud of him then and now, but I missed him a lot.

I worried about him, too. I worried he was afraid or sad. I worried about what he had to do over there and how he would feel about it. But my biggest fear was he would come back to us wounded—maybe missing an arm or a leg—or worse, that he would not come back to us at all. I didn't know how Mom and I would deal with that. I didn't know if we could. We never talked about that fear, but both of us knew it was there. It lived with us all the time, invisible but present, like a ghost. Sometimes, we could ignore it, but at others, it would pop up and scare us.

Maybe that was why I was angry. Not angry at Dad—it wasn't his fault—but angry he had to go, that he had to be apart from us while other guys' fathers remained behind safe and secure, cheering their sons on at soccer games, talking with their sons' teachers at school conferences, working together raking leaves or washing the car, all that stuff. It was unfair that Dad had to go, and they didn't.

With all that going on, plus the Ama and Sean thing, plus Mom's problems with the mayor, I had a lot on my plate. Still, Budge had nothing to do with it. None of it was his fault. He just happened to be in the wrong place at the wrong time. I wasn't so sure about Evie, though. After all, she was Ama's best friend. As for Mike and Sean, well, they weren't that close to me. Mike was alright, but Sean could drop off the face of the earth and I wouldn't throw him a rope.

By the time I got home I decided I owed Budge an apology. I went into the kitchen, took out a string cheese from the refrigerator and sat on the couch in the living room. I took out my cell phone and while nibbling on the cheese texted him a message.

SUP BUDGE, I wrote. I guessed he wouldn't be able to answer me for a while if he was at the doctor's so I asked him to text me back: TMB. I hoped he would.

An hour later he did text me. NADA U?

SAME. JUST THINKING.

WITH WHAT? Budge replied.

Okay, so he was still cheesed off with me. Maybe I deserved that. GOOD ONE, DUDE, I said.

I waited for him to answer but it seemed like he was taking a long time; I caved. SO HOWD IT GO @ THE DOC?

MEH.

Meh? I could almost see him shrugging his shoulders in that I-don't-care way of his. Budge could keep things to himself when he wanted to and that worried me sometimes. He was *still* my best friend, even if I had treated him like dirt.

WASSUP DOCWISE?

NOT SUPPOSED 2 SHOOT HOOPS.

Budge wasn't a wimp, I knew that, but I also knew that Merv would ground him if he knew his son was doing almost anything physical. Like shooting hoops in my driveway.

As if reading my mind, he texted, MERV WOULD KILL ME.

Strange how those words hit me, like a warning or something. Not that his father would kill him; Merv was strict, but he wasn't a psycho. That's not what worried me. I just felt that maybe Budge could drop out of my life unexpectedly. A scary thought. I stopped texting him and called him instead.

"So, listen," I said, before he could speak, "you know I was in kind of a bad mood yesterday."

"Really, Captain Obvious?" Budge said.

I sighed. "Yeah, really. You know you're my best friend, right?"

"You mean your only friend?"

I laughed despite myself. "Fine. You can mind my business if you want."

There was a pause, but I could hear him breathing. Finally, Budge said, "I've got your back, dude. Always."

And that was that.

14

WHILE ALL THIS DRAMA was going on in my life, the Braves had advanced to the semi-finals in the city soccer league. Game day was Saturday. Mom drove me to the field, wearing her lucky Cincinnati Reds hat—why she thought it was lucky for soccer, I never knew. Dad would tease her no end about it.

I wondered if Budge was going to come to the game, but then I remembered the girls were supposed to work on the bird blind that weekend. I didn't see him, but there was still some time before the game started and Budge was not famous for being on time for anything. I knew we were buds again so I figured he'd show up in his own sweet Budge-time.

A few moments later the referee blew his whistle, and the game was on.

The Titans were fast, and they scored the first goal just seconds before half-time. I wiped the sweat out of my eyes with my shirtsleeve and got a drink of water. I scanned the crowd and found Budge sitting on the grass along the sidelines. I smiled and waved at him, but he didn't see me.

Of course, the person I missed most at the game was Dad. He would have been passing out water right now or giving encouragement to the players. He might be keeping the stats. He would do basically anything Coach asked him to. I wished he were there.

About twelve minutes into the second half, we tied the score. We high-fived each other and grinned as we jogged back to the center of the field.

There probably wasn't much more than two minutes left to play when a Brave launched a high blooper of a kick toward the goal. I saw the ball floating down big as the moon in my eyes. I saw the keeper stretch up his arms, saw the ball coming down and, without knowing exactly how I did it, I leapt into the air, snapping my head forward. The Titans keeper jumped for the ball at the same time. We collided full force. His shoulder slammed into my chest and the next thing I knew, I was upside down, sailing over his shoulder.

I hit the ground hard and felt the air whoosh out of me. I lay there stunned. I don't remember if I blacked out or not, but suddenly, there was Coach and a few of the other guys helping me to my feet. They were grinning like crazy and patting me on the back. Then I noticed not only had I landed inside the net, but so had the ball.

That was game. Two to one.

I wish Dad could have seen that!

15

ONCE THE EXCITEMENT of winning the game wore off, the pain set in—it took all of ten minutes. I must have thrown my hands out to break my fall when I crashed into the Titans keeper and now my left wrist was red and swollen. Hurt like crazy.

"Can you wiggle your fingers?" Coach asked me. I must have been dizzy; I thought he asked me if I could wiggle my ears. I could move my fingers, but just barely. I winced. "That's good," Coach said, gently holding my forearm.

Easy for him to say.

Mom stood close by, looking on, a worried expression on her face. "Is it broken?"

"I'm not sure," said Coach. "It might be. You should probably take him to the ER and have it checked."

"Okay. Come on, Sweetie." She put her arm around my shoulders. Even though she looked worried, she was cool about it all.

Coach patted me on the back as we walked off the field. "Great game, Haycorn."

It *was* a great game. There was something awesomely cool about walking off the field as an injured champion. My wrist hurt; that wasn't cool, but I thought if I wound up with a cast or something, that would make up for the pain. Like a soldier getting a Purple Heart. There would be pain, but you'd also have a medal to flash around and a story everyone would want to hear.

The emergency room at Bethesda North Hospital was not busy, so we didn't have to wait long before we saw a doctor. He sent me to get x-rays, but he was already certain that I had fractured my wrist. An hour and a half later I walked out of the hospital with my left wrist wrapped in a splint. The doctor said I would have to wear the splint a few weeks until the fracture healed.

All the way home I kept looking at the splint and smiled. *How cool is this?* I couldn't wait for the other kids to see it. Mom went on saying how sorry she was I had gotten hurt, as if it was her fault or she could have prevented it. I only half-heard what she was saying because I was thinking about the story I would tell my friends. *Awesome.*

The doctor told me to take it easy and rest for the remainder of the day. That was okay with me since I was feeling sleepy anyway. Mom said it was probably from the pain pill the doctor gave me. Fine, there would be plenty of time later for me to show off my injury. I lay on the couch, my left arm across my chest, surfing through the channels on TV, while Mom worked in the kitchen making me something to eat.

A sky full of airplanes dumping out streams of bombs appeared on television. The picture was in black and white and was grainy, and I immediately recognized a History Channel program, World War II no doubt. Dad, the former history teacher, loves the History Channel and watches it all the time. He tries to get me interested in it and I would watch it with him sometimes—especially the World War II stuff, since Grandpa Smith had been in the war—but after a while it bores me. I mean, how many programs about Hitler can a guy watch?

As I lay there half awake, watching planes spiraling down out of the sky trailing black smoke and flame, I thought of Dad. The thought struck me that maybe sometime in the future he might be part of a History Channel program about the war in Afghanistan. Surely, there would be such a program. He might be one of the many nameless soldiers you see marching in long columns across a desert, or maybe speeding through a village in a convoy of Humvees, or maybe pinned down behind sandbags shooting at an enemy they couldn't see. Dad would think it funny; instead of watching the History Channel, he would be acting in it.

Of course, "acting" wasn't really the right word. He was in the war for real. Still, it would be wild to see him on TV. Maybe I'd be telling my own kids, *Look, there's Grandpa!* and he would be surprised to see himself in the program. But I wondered about some of the other soldiers in my imaginary program. Some of them would have died in the war. What would their children say when they saw that program, and for a few seconds their fathers were once again alive and well?

Jeezul. That would really suck.

I fell asleep with that thought in my mind and had crazy dreams where guys wearing turbans goose-stepped down a street beneath flags that had pictures of Yankees' shortstop Derek Jeter on them—I have no idea why. There was other weird stuff, too, that I can't remember in detail. When I woke up, the room was dark, and the television was turned off.

"Mom?" Using my right arm, I pushed myself up to a sitting position.

She must have been in the study because she heard me without me having to call her a second time. "How are you feeling?" she said, coming into the room and sitting on the couch beside me.

"It hurts." It really did; heat and throbbing pain were pulsing through my arm.

"I'm sure it does." She looked at her watch. "It's time. We can give you some aspirin."

I had slept for almost five hours. Mom asked if I was hungry. I requested my favorite, grilled cheese and tomato sandwich. "Not Velveeta. Real cheese."

While she was making my sandwich, I switched on the television again. The History Channel came on, right where I had left it, but this time I was watching the credits for one program scroll by while a voice-over promoted the next two programs. They didn't sound all that interesting, but I thought I'd watch them anyway, thinking maybe they were programs Dad would watch.

Mom brought in the sandwich and sat with me. "What are we watching?"

"History Channel."

"Your father's favorite."

The program was lame—no guns, no war—but we watched it anyway, maybe as a way of remembering Dad. The program was about political scandals and payoffs and talked about some guy named Boss Tweed and something called Teapot Dome and other stuff I had never heard about. It was getting really boring and I was about to switch to another channel, but Mom stopped me.

"Wait, Hay, leave it on."

I rolled my eyes. "You've got to be kidding."

"No, let's watch."

I sighed and took a bite of my sandwich. I tried to get interested in the program, but I couldn't. Mom, though, was paying attention. Finally, just when I thought it would never end, the program was over.

"About time. I was almost asleep again."

She laughed. "It wasn't that bad, and it gave me an idea."

"An idea for what?"

"A way that I could find out if the mayor really took a bribe to get the velodrome approved."

"Seriously?" I should have paid closer attention. "You got that from TV?"

"In all those scandals it seemed there was always someone who threatened to reveal everything. Maybe that person went to the press or the police with what they knew, or maybe they were on the inside, part of the scandal and wanted a bigger piece of the pie."

"I don't get it. How does that help you? Wait! What if we found a person like that? Someone who could shake up the mayor and make him think his plan was coming apart. But there was only the mayor and Mr. Ambrose at the castle, so who would this mystery someone be?"

She looked at me and grinned. "Me."

16

T HAT WAS ALL SHE SAID. I didn't know what she meant and
when I asked her to explain, she said that I should leave
things up to her.

"It's a problem for adults now," she said. "I don't want you
involved."

Really? Adults? How about *adult*, as in the singular? And if
it wasn't for me and Budge, no *adult* would know anything about
the ghost or what was going on at the castle.

I didn't sleep well that night and it wasn't because of my broken
wrist. Mom was up to something. I couldn't get my mind off it. The
smile on her face after watching the History Channel flashed in my
brain. It was a sly smile—not her usual, warm smile—and I was
suspicious of it. She was cooking up some scheme, alright, and it was
killing me not knowing what it was all about. I was certain she was
going after Mayor Davenport, and she was going it alone. Mom is
smart, but still, she's just one woman. I worried that she was getting

herself into a jam and that I wouldn't be able to help her. What would Dad do? He said I was the man of the house while he was away, and I knew he wouldn't want me leaving Mom hanging out there on her own. No, I had to do something.

I finally fell asleep, my mind full of worries.

The next morning, Budge texted me. He wanted to hang out, and half an hour later he was knocking on our door.

His eyes grew wide when he saw the splint on my arm. "Jeezul, Hay, what did you do?"

I thought he would have known about my injury but then I remembered I only saw him at a distance on game day. He didn't really hang with the guys on the soccer team, so I could see where he might not have heard about my injured wrist. We went onto the deck at the back of the house, and I told him everything.

He whistled in appreciation. "Freaking awesome. And your goal was something else. We thought you were dead."

I laughed. "So did I. That goalie knocked the stuffing out of me."

He nodded. "Yeah, he was a big dude."

We sat on the deck and watched a pair of goldfinches eating seeds from one of Mom's bird feeders. After a while he said, "I was thinking of going over to the preserve today. Do you want to come?" He didn't look at me but continued watching the birds.

I had forgotten all about Ama's group working on the bird blind that weekend. My first thought was, *Jeezul no, why would I want to do that?* but then I thought how cool it would be to show off my splint to everyone. I could already see the expression on that loudmouth Sean's froggy face as everyone crowded around me, the wounded hero. But there was something else we needed to talk about.

I lowered my voice so Mom wouldn't hear if she came out. "Listen, Budge, my mom's up to something. About the castle. I think she's going after Mr. Davenport, but she won't tell me what she's doing; says it's a grown-up's job."

"So?"

"So, she might get in trouble."

"She can go to the police," Budge said.

I shook my head. "No way, that's not how she rolls. Mom can be stubborn; my father says that all the time. She'll try it— whatever *it* may be—on her own. She says, 'If you want a job done right, do it yourself.'"

"Sounds dumb," Budge said, then, "No offense."

"That's why we have to do something."

Budge looked worried. "Hmm, not sure about that, Hay."

"What if it was your mother we were talking about?"

He drummed his fingers on the armrest as if giving the idea some thought. "Well, my mother, yes," he said. "My sisters not so much." He looked around, his eyes wide as if he thought someone was spying on us. "Okay, what's your plan?"

"I don't know."

"Sounds foolproof, dude," Budge said.

"I'll come up with something; I have to! But are you in or out?"

"I said I had your back, remember? Yeah, I'm in."

I slapped his back. "Thanks, man."

"You know, we could think about it as we go to the nature preserve."

"You're pretty eager for that, Budge. I'm surprised." He didn't answer, but his face turned red, and he looked away. "Alright, let's go. But I can't ride, you know," I said, holding up my injured arm.

"So, we'll walk," he said, excitedly. "It's not that far."

I was glad to see Budge smile. Maybe we were back to where we were before I ticked him off. "Sure," I said.

Mom didn't want me to stay at the preserve too long, saying I still needed to rest. I promised her I would be back soon. When we got there, we saw several cars in the VFW parking lot next to the preserve. They belonged to the parents of the kids in the environmental group. As we walked down the path into the preserve, we heard hammers banging and saws snoring among the trees.

We rounded a bend in the path. Some people were working on a wood-frame structure off to the side. Four posts were set in the ground and a couple men, including Dr. Yendi, Ama's father, were nailing horizontal boards between them. Ama and Evie, wearing shorts and their green club shirts, knelt on the ground, a tape measure stretched between them. Off to the side, Sean and Mike sawed boards placed across two sawhorses.

One of the other girls saw us coming up the path and called to Ama. She looked up and rose to her feet. Dirt clung to her knees. A wayward strand of hair fell across one eye. She brushed it away with the back of her hand.

"Hey, Budge," she called. "Hello, Haycorn."

Her greeting to me was not as friendly as I would have liked, but then again, Sean was right there. Then, she noticed the splint on my arm.

"Oh, my gosh! What happened to you?"

She and Evie and some of the other girls crowded around me, asking, "*Does it hurt? Is it broken?* and a bunch of other questions. It was great.

"That looks painful." When I looked into Ama's dark brown eyes, I saw her concern.

I shrugged. "Maybe just a little," I said, although by now that earlier pain pill had worn off and my wrist was starting to sing a nasty song about hurt.

Budge stood there grinning, enjoying the popularity I was receiving, since he was my best friend and, so, popular as well. Sean and Mike came over to see what was going on. Mike played sweeper for the Hornets and had been at the game. The splint impressed him. Sean, on the other hand, stood looking at my wrist with a stunned expression. I could imagine him thinking, *How am I going to top that?*

"What happened?" Ama repeated. I explained to everyone how I had scored the winning goal and had been nobly injured on the field of battle.

"You should have seen it," Mike said. "Haycorn did a somersault right over the goalie."

Ama smiled up at me, finally.

"Too bad you didn't land on your head," Sean said. "It's so thick you wouldn't have gotten hurt." He snorted a little laugh.

I was about ready to pop him, even with one hand, but Ama spoke up before I could.

"Be quiet, Sean. Can't you see that he's hurt?"

Wow! Ama had my back! If my wrist still hurt, I didn't feel it. I put on my best sad puppy look. Sean's face turned as red his Cincinnati Reds cap.

"Did you guys finish cutting those boards?" she said. "It would be great if you could get that done." She showed them a big, fake smile.

Sean shuffled off. I could almost see smoke coming out of his ears. Mike shrugged, picked up a saw, and joined Sean.

Budge and Evie were talking off to one side and the others had returned to their work.

"Thanks for the support," I said.

She looked away. "No big deal."

But *I* thought it was. I tagged along beside her as she started slowly walking down the path.

"I'm not sure you deserved it," Ama said.

I stopped. "Why not? What do you mean?"

Her eyes narrowed. "You've been pretty mean lately, Haycorn. First, you promise to help us, then you get all fussy about something and you start ignoring us. What's with that?"

"What's with *that*? What's with you and Sean?" The words were no sooner out of my mouth than I wanted to cram them back in. The angry look on Ama's face told me I had made a mistake. A big mistake.

She stepped close to me. "What are you talking about?" Those soft, dark eyes had turned hard.

Once again, I could see myself—as though I was watching a movie—acting like an idiot, but I couldn't stop the film. "You and Sean, as in Ama and Sean are an item, as in boyfriend and girlfriend."

She glared at me, folding her arms across her chest. In a calm, but deadly voice, she said, "And where did you hear that?"

"Mike said you let Sean touch your boob."

I never saw it coming. She slapped me so hard, I felt the jolt clear down to my wrist.

"Liar!" Tears formed in her eyes. "That's not true! I never."

I rubbed the side of my face with my good hand. "What are you slapping *me* for? I didn't say it, Sean did!"

"Perv!" She was crying now. "You and Sean, both of you. Pervs!" She quickly wiped away her tears. "That's how much you know. Sean was never my boyfriend! He can lie as much as he wants to, but we were never an *item*."

She turned and stomped back up the path.

"Ama!" She didn't turn around. All I could think was two things: one, I wouldn't want to be Sean right then and, two, I wasn't so happy being Haycorn, either.

Budge saw me standing on the path and walked back to me. "So, you two were talking?" he said, smiling. "How did it go?"

"My wrist is killing me. I need to go home."

His smile disappeared. "Sure, Hay, no problem." He didn't ask anything more.

As we walked home, every step shot bullets of pain through my wrist. I deserved them all for what I had said to Ama. I couldn't understand how every time I opened my mouth, even with good intentions, I always seemed to screw things up. I decided I was truly the world's biggest jerk.

I barely said two words to Mom when I got home. She could tell something was wrong, but she probably thought it was my wrist that was bugging me. After she gave me another pain pill, I went to my room to lie down.

As I stared up at the ceiling, Ama's face appeared before me, her smile and bright eyes making me smile, but only until the moment I heard myself repeating those awful words. *What an idiot!* She had defended me when Sean dissed me. That should have told me something. Should have given me a clue that maybe she did like me after all. But no. Idiot me had to push it, had to make things worse. How could I have said that? It wasn't the first time my big mouth had gotten me in trouble and it probably wouldn't be the last. The only thing that made me feel better is what I imagined she had said to Sean. *Jeezul-Pete!*

17

I NEEDED TO MAKE THINGS RIGHT with Ama. I needed to apologize. I got up and went to my desk, took a pen from the drawer, a sheet of paper from my notebook, and started to write her a note. The funny thing about me was that my big mouth was always quick to speak and often said the wrong things at the wrong time, but when I wrote, I had time to think things through, to think about what I really wanted to say. While I wasn't the brightest student in the class, I did have an ability to write pretty well. It came easily to me and English was my favorite subject, if I could say *any* class was a favorite. I gave careful thought to what I wanted to tell her.

I didn't want to write a mushy love letter, even if I'd known how. But I did want to tell Ama that I didn't mean to hurt her, that I wanted us to be friends, and was sorry for my words—and actions—and was really sorry I was such a dumb jerk. I wrote:

Ama, I'm really not a perv, but I can sometimes be a dumb jerk. (I underlined that last part just to make sure she got the point.) *I'm sorry for saying, well you know, what I said. You're smart and funny. Pretty. I shouldn't have listened to what another dumb jerk said about you. He lied; I know that. Anyway, I wouldn't blame you if you tore up this note in a million pieces and used it to line a gerbil cage—do you have a gerbil?—but I hope you won't. I hope we can still be friends.*

Sincerely,
Haycorn Smith

I folded the letter in thirds, tucked it in a lavender envelope I found in Mom's desk, and wrote *Ama* on the outside. *Here goes nothing*, I thought.

•　　　•　　　•

The doctor had told Mom to keep me home from school for a couple days to let me rest, so I texted Budge and asked him to come to the house the next morning before school to do me a favor.

I hid the envelope in my math book, the last place anyone would ever find it, if anyone were even looking for it. It was definitely the last place *I* would look since I avoided opening any math book, if at all possible, afraid of letting all those numbers run loose in my room. They were out to divide and subtract me.

But my greater fear was how Ama would react to my letter. Would she still be angry and ignore it? Would it calm her down, as I hoped it would? And if she liked it, would she read between the lines? Did she think I liked her as a girlfriend? I mean, I did, sort of, but did I want her to know that?

I looked out the window and saw Budge coming up the walk. I pulled the letter out of the book and ran downstairs. He was already on the porch by the time I got there and opened the door.

"A letter?" Budge said, when I handed it to him. He held it at arms-length as though it was a snake about to bite him.

"Yeah, you know, words on paper," I said. "Hand-written."

"Wow! What will they think of next?" He grinned. "For Ama?"

"What's it say on the envelope?"

"For Ama."

"That's your first clue," I said.

"Okay, Haycorn, sure. I can do this. No problem."

He turned as if to go, then stopped and held the envelope to his nose.

"Jeezul, Budge! What are you doing?"

"I just want to see if it smelled. You know, perfume."

"There's no perfume. Just get it out of your nose, will you?"

He nodded and put the envelope in his backpack. "How's the arm?"

"Wrist," I said.

"How's the wrist?"

"Okay, I guess," I said, leaning against the door. "Hurts sometimes, but I'll live."

"Good," Budge said. He stepped off the porch. "Got to get going."

"Right." He started down the walk. "Hey, Budge!"

He turned.

"Thanks," I said.

"Sure. Keep your fingers crossed," he said, over his shoulder as he walked down the sidewalk.

And I did, even the fingers of my injured hand.

18

MOM WENT TO WORK while I stayed home from school, trying hard not to imagine Budge handing Ama my note. What would she say? Would she even accept it? I turned on the TV to take my mind off things and switched between ghost hunting programs on Syfy and World War II programs on the History Channel. Both channels were boring—reruns as usual—but I watched a few of the ghost programs again. I kept looking for hidden wires, or a suspicious hand in the picture to explain some of the stuff that was going on, although honestly, if you sat down and analyzed each show, there really wasn't much going on. Sure, the ghosthunters would give each other frightened looks and say, *What was that? Did you hear that?* or one of the girls might get startled and squeal with fright, but most of the time, things were pretty tame. Maybe even lame.

I had another reason for watching the shows, though, and that was Harry, our own local ghost. Despite everything going on in my life, I had not forgotten about him. It's just that with Mom declaring Loveland Castle off-limits, I couldn't do anything more about him.

Still, I thought about him.

Had Budge and I really contacted the spirit of Harry Andrews, the builder of the castle? Why did he make himself known to us? There is a theory that ghosts hang around for a reason. Maybe they have some unfinished business—they didn't get to say goodbye to their children, or they want to tell their relatives where they had placed their wills, or they want to make sure their grandchildren get on the school bus on time, whatever. Maybe they don't even know they are dead and, so, remain in their homes wondering who all these new, strange people are, tromping around in their living room.

What was Harry's story? Did he not know he was dead as a doornail? If he did know then why was he still haunting the castle? Shouldn't he be somewhere else? Heaven? The other place?

I played back in my mind the last two visits me and Budge had made to the castle. The first time, when we had recorded the mayor and Mister Ambrose, we heard Harry—at least we believed it was Harry—say, *Leave me.* That made sense to me. The ghost probably didn't want a couple crooks in his castle. But the second time …

I got up off the couch and went into the study. Mom's digital recorder sat on the desk. I picked it up and fiddled with it until I found the track we had recorded when we were last at the castle. I got goosebumps just listening to me and Budge talk and hearing Budge's surprise when something touched him and the room suddenly turned icy cold. Then, there was that voice again. A shiver like a fast spider ran down my back as I heard, *the wall.*

I took the recorder back to the couch and replayed it several times, holding it right against my ear, hoping to hear other words or sounds, any clue that would help me understand what the ghost was talking about. There was nothing more.

The ghost program on the TV was over, and now some guy with a big, bushy moustache was poking around in a dark basement with a flashlight. I put down the recorder. The guy said something about the old-time gangster Al Capone and I turned up the volume. He was talking directly to the camera in a serious but excited voice. Apparently, someone had discovered Capone's safe in that basement. It had been hidden for years in the wall. *The wall.* The safe was locked and now, for the first time since Al Capone had locked it, the reporter—with the help of some other guys that actually knew what they were doing—was going to open the safe live on TV. After many minutes of boring work on the safe, and non-stop chatter from the reporter, the door fell open. Empty.

The wall. Could that be what Harry meant? The ghost must know everything that goes on in his castle. He must see every Knight working there, every visitor. He certainly saw the two guys with the money—and didn't like what he saw. After Mister Ambrose drove away, Budge and I saw the mayor go back into the castle with that case, the case we believed was full of money, but he came back out empty-handed! That must be what Harry meant—the money is hidden in the castle wall!

I knew I shouldn't bother her at work, but I thought she needed to know right away. I texted Mom: I FOUND THE MONEY.

Right away she replied: ?

THE MONEY IN THE CASE. I hated spelling every single word out for her, but she had never learned how to text the proper way.

SAY NO MORE. STAY PUT. I'M ON MY WAY HOME

I thought about texting Budge, but I was too chicken to do that. I was afraid he would have bad news about my letter to Ama. I was supposed to rest, to sleep if I could, but I was too wound up to sleep. My wrist throbbed a little, not too much, but I was too excited to think about it. One-handed, I slapped together a peanut butter and jelly sandwich and ate it, pacing around the house, looking for something to do, something to keep me busy until Mom came home. I played Minecraft on my computer for a while, I didn't know how long, until I heard the doorbell ring.

Mom! I jumped up but then realized she would never ring the bell of her own house.

I went to the door and opened it. *Whoa!* Ama stood on the step, a slight smile upon her face. She didn't look directly at me, her gaze sliding just past my ear.

"I brought your homework."

I stood there for a minute, just looking at her. She had never been to our house before.

She shifted from one foot to another and finally, I snapped out of it. "Oh, thanks. Do you want to come in?"

"I don't think so," she said, looking at me. "My mother's waiting for me."

That's when I noticed the SUV at the curb. Mrs. Yendi sat behind the wheel.

"Okay." I stepped out onto the front porch with her.

"It's not much, really." She dug into her backpack and pulled out a few sheets of paper. She handed them to me. Our fingers almost touched.

"Thanks."

We stood there awhile not really looking at each other, except for a glance now and then. I heard a school bus somewhere in the distance. A late-season cicada sang from a tree.

"Ama ..."

She looked up. "Budge gave me your note," she said in a rush.

"Oh?" *Clever comeback, Haycorn.*

She nodded. "It was very nice. You have really good penmanship."

"Thanks."

"How's your wrist?"

I shrugged. "Okay." *Speak, Haycorn, speak.*

"I'm sorry I slapped you."

I waved my good hand, as though shooing away a fly. "Yeah, well, I deserved it. I never should have said what I said."

"You do know Sean is not my boyfriend, don't you?"

"Yes."

"Okay." She looked around as though realizing for the first time that she was standing on my porch and that fact seemed to daze her. "Will you be in school tomorrow?" she said, turning back to me.

"I'm not sure. Maybe."

"If you're not, I'll get your homework for you again."

I smiled. "Cool. Thanks a lot."

She stepped off the porch. "See you, Hay."

She walked out to her mother's SUV. She got in and waved as the van pulled away. I stood there on the porch watching it drive down the street, realizing for the first time that I wasn't wearing shoes.

No sooner had I gone back inside than Mom came home. She swept into the living room. "Okay, tell me everything," she said, dropping her briefcase on the sofa. "Where's the money?"

I explained my theory to her. She looked thoughtful. "Hmm, that could work. The mayor must have thought it all out beforehand, though. It's unlikely that he dug a hole in a stone wall in the few minutes you and Budge saw him."

"Unless he was Superman."

She ignored my joke. "It seems odd that he would hide the money in such a public place, but then again, maybe that's the last place anyone would think to look. I don't think he would keep it there for a long time. He may have already recovered it for all we know."

"So, what now?" She looked at me in a way that told me she was seeing me but not seeing me. She was lost in her own thoughts, and she wasn't including me. "Mom?"

When she brushes me off like that—and she has done it plenty of times before—I know there is no sense pushing her. She could be stubborn at times. Dad says that often enough. I knew what was going on. She had already told me she would take care of the mayor and I was not to get involved. I was afraid she was now about to spring whatever trap she had set for him.

That night I received an email from Dad. As usual, he couldn't say a lot because of security reasons, but it was great to hear from him. He did say things had been relatively peaceful where he was stationed, but my imagination blew up the "relatively" part and I thought he was trying to put the best face on a bad situation. I didn't know if that was true or not, but the nightly news programs and the Internet posted so many terrible stories about Afghanistan, I thought being there must truly be like being in Hell. He was sparing us all the bad stuff. He reminded me, as he always did, I was the "man of the house" while he was away. I should be good and take care of Mom. He was counting on me.

I wanted to tell him I was worried about her. She could be getting herself into trouble, I wanted to say, but I didn't. I wanted to ask him what I should do, but I couldn't. I told him about the simple things, the easy things: school, soccer. I didn't think my fractured wrist would be a big deal to him, so I told him about it. Told him what Budge and me had been up to, stuff like that. I even told him about the girls building the bird blind.

It was only an email, but somehow it made me feel connected to him. I missed his advice, something I'm not sure I would ever tell him to his face, but seeing his words on my computer screen made me feel better. There wasn't any real advice written there for me, but his words said he was counting on me and was proud of the job I was doing. Okay, so I must be doing something right.

19

I TALKED MOM INTO allowing me to go to school the next day. Normally, I would be trying to get another day off, but now that I had patched things up with Budge and Ama—especially Ama—I was eager to get back. My wrist didn't hurt all that much now anyway, so why not?

Evie Parker walked by as I was pulling some books from my locker. "Hi, Haycorn," she said, smiling. So, if Evie was talking to me then Ama had spread the word among her friends; Haycorn was a good guy, don't freeze him out.

Even better, Ama spoke to me in home room as soon as I saw her. "How's your arm feeling?"

"Better. The swelling's gone down and the doctor is supposed to cast it on Friday. I'll let you be the first to sign the cast."

She laughed. "Okay, I'll think up something funny to say. Maybe I'll draw a cartoon."

She was a pretty good artist. "That would be cool."

She put her backpack on the floor and sat at her desk. We still had a few minutes before the bell rang. "We're more than halfway finished with the bird blind," she said, looking up at me, "but we still have more work to do. Do you want to help?" I lifted my arm wrapped in the splint. "Oh, duh, your arm. Of course, you can't help."

"No, I can help. Maybe I can't do heavy stuff, but I should be able to do something." I knew I was already benched for the soccer finals because of my injury, and I felt bad about that, letting the team down. I didn't want to let her down, too.

"Are you sure? I don't want you to hurt yourself even more."

"I'm sure."

"Great. We'll be there on Saturday morning. Around ten?"

"Fine with me," I said, just as the class bell rang. I walked to my desk a happy man.

There was a school assembly that morning. We didn't know about it ahead of time, but that was okay. The assemblies took us out of class, and that was all that mattered. Even one of those lame school band concerts was better than class.

I saw Sean Baer in the hall as we filed into the auditorium. He gave me a hard stare and then looked around to make sure no teachers were there before flipping me the bird. I grinned back, sure now that Ama had told him off, and that seemed to make him angrier. *Get over it, Sean, you loser.*

After the principal reminded us we should be on our best behavior for our visitors, a trumpet sounded from the back of the auditorium. Of course, we all turned around to see what was going on. No one ever blew a trumpet during an assembly. Keith Burton, one of the band geeks, stood there in the aisle, his trumpet in hand. He raised it to his lips once more, blew a few more sour notes, and then stood aside. From the lobby, a procession of knights slowly walked down the aisle toward the stage.

Budge sat beside me. We looked at each other. Knights? I shrugged.

The guy leading the parade wore a blue cloak and carried a big red banner with gold letters that spelled out *KOGT*: Knights of the Golden Trail. They were the keepers of Chateau Laroche, Harry's knights. Eight men, most of them as old as Dad, if not older, followed the guy with the flag. They wore brightly colored tunics and cloaks over armor that covered their arms and legs. They clanked when they walked. Helmets of different shapes and styles—I swear some of them must have been old paint cans—topped their costumes. Each man carried a fake sword.

"What are they doing here?" Budge whispered.

"Beats me." *This is weird.* Here I had just been thinking about the ghost and the castle and how Budge and me should go back and see if we could make contact with Harry again, when his knights show up and parade right before our eyes. At our school no less. *Weird.*

"Geez, they're slow," Budge said.

"Yeah, I guess they can't see too well through those big tin cans on their heads."

Finally, the band of knights made it on stage, although one of them stumbled on the steps leading up to it and almost fell off. Some of the kids laughed. I felt sorry for the guy.

One of the men stepped up to the microphone and lifted the visor of his helmet. He wore glasses under his helmet, but he was too far away for me to make out any other details.

"Good morning, kind sirs and gentle ladies. My name is Sir Jack."

I looked at Budge. *Sir Jack?* I mouthed. He grinned.

Sir Jack promised a demonstration of a medieval tournament right after he read an important notice. While the knights waved their swords behind him to warm up, Sir Jack unrolled a large scroll on the podium and read from it. Full of knight-talk, a lot of "thees and thous," but the bottom line was, the knights were going to host a Medieval Month at the castle, a series of public programs about the good old days when, as Sir Jack said, "Manly knights did battle fire-breathing dragons," or "entered the lists"— whatever they were—"for the favor of their ladies fair."

Sir Jack said the kick-off for the month would begin the very next day. It would be a day of music, food, and "revelry and mortal combat"— again, Sir Jack's words. The knight encouraged our teachers to bring their students to the events and asked the students to tell their parents about it. While he spoke, a couple teachers were passing out Medieval Month flyers to the students.

It hit me right away: *The festivities will start tomorrow!* What about the money hidden in the castle? The mayor would have to go and get it, wouldn't he? He couldn't risk having all those people running around in the castle if the money was still there, could he?

I poked Budge and leaned toward him. The knights on stage were now in full combat mode, running around whacking each other with their fake swords. I whispered my suspicions to him.

"Jeezul, Hay, we've got to catch the mayor taking the money."

I nodded. "My thoughts, exactly."

Three of the knights lay unmoving on the stage, apparently "dead," but the remaining five still banged away at each other. Their swords clanged and crashed on armor, sounding like my Dad hammering out a dented fender. Sir Jack had told us to cheer on the knights we liked best as they fought each other. The students clapped and cheered, but loudly booed one guy in black who kept sneaking around behind the other knights, striking them in the back. That's the kind of knight Sean would be, I thought. A back-stabber.

But I wasn't paying all that much attention to the knights. I was too busy thinking about other things.

"You think I can sleep over at your house tonight?" I said to Budge. "I've got a plan."

He shot me a worried look. "A plan?"

He didn't always like my plans. Too much stress on his heart, I guess.

When I got home from school there was a copy of the *Loveland Herald* on the porch. I brought it inside and opened it. A color photo of Sir Jack and other knights, wearing their knight costumes, and standing in front of Chateau Laroche, splashed across the page. The misspelled headline read "Mid-evil Month Merriment and Mayhem." The article talked about the castle and listed all the upcoming events in a sidebar. The newspaper confirmed tomorrow as the day everything would start. There was no mention of a ghost at the castle, and I wondered if the knights even knew Harry still lived there.

Okay, so now I knew I had to act that night, no matter what Mom had said about the castle being off-limits. *It's an adult thing, Haycorn,* she had said. *I don't want you getting involved.* Maybe it was an adult thing, but wasn't I an adult? Dad had said I was the man of the house while he was away. How could I be that man if I wasn't an adult? And if Dad were here, wouldn't he be doing the same thing I was planning on doing? Helping Mom? Yes, he would.

The moment she walked in the door from work, and before she had a chance to read the newspaper, I asked her if I could spend the night at Budge's house.

"But it's a school night, Hay."

"I know, it's just that Budge and me are working on this, uh, paper together. It's a special project kind of thing, and we really need to get it done soon. Please?"

"Budge's mom is okay with this?"

"Sure." Budge's mother was a push-over and she loved me. I was certain it would be okay with her.

"Well, I guess if it's alright with her ..."

"Thanks, Mom."

"Just make sure to take your pain medicine with you and try not to stay up too late."

I wasn't worried about the pain medicine since I only had to take it as needed and the pain wasn't really all that bad any more. Quickly, before Mom had the chance to change her mind, I grabbed my books and the other things I would need to put my plan into action and stuffed them all into my backpack. She offered to drive me to Budge's house, but he didn't live far from our house so I decided to walk. I didn't want her to change her mind on the ride over.

Despite its cookie-cutter style, Budge's house stood out from the others. With five kids living there, the house looked worn out. Like it wanted to cry. A couple bikes were thrown on the lawn. A card table sat on the porch, piled with books and papers; I didn't know why. A garden hose lay tangled alongside the driveway. Budge's parents each had a car parked in the driveway and his older sister Karen parked her beat-up Escort in the street in front of the house. Usually, there were one or two of her friends' clunkers parked there, too.

There were always a lot of kids at his house. His four sisters, their girlfriends, and all the guys who hung out there because of all the girls. It was no wonder Budge spent so much time at my house. The poor guy had nowhere else to go for some peace and quiet.

Budge was sitting on the couch with his sister Rachel and some guy I didn't know; her boyfriend, I guessed. Budge got up when I entered the room and we headed for his bedroom.

Before we could get there, though, Mrs. Shifflet came out of the kitchen and, seeing me, gave me a big hug. She nearly crushed the life out of me. Mrs. Shifflet is a big woman, tall like Budge, but solid, an Amazon of a woman.

"Watch out for his arm, Ma," Budge said, and she immediately let me go.

"Oh, did I hurt you?" She looked worried.

"No, ma'am, I'm fine."

She seemed relieved. She wore old-fashioned horn-rimmed glasses that kept sliding down her nose. She pushed them up. "Will you have dinner with us?"

"Haycorn's spending the night, Ma," Budge said.

"Oh, that's fine."

She *was* easy, I thought, but a nice person anyway.

We shut the door to his bedroom and kept our voices low. Too many ears in the house. We sat on the floor as I explained my plan to trap the mayor and find the money.

"We'll be just like the ghosthunters," I said. "We'll hide a recorder in the stables. All we have to do is record the mayor's voice when he goes back to the castle for the money."

"What if he's alone?"

"What do you mean?"

"If he's alone, he won't be talking to anyone unless he talks to himself all the time. There won't be any voice to record," Budge said.

I hate it when Budge is right, but he did have a point. "Hmm, okay, maybe. I guess we need to get him on video, too."

"Yeah, sure dude, that'll work," Budge said, with a smirk. "Uh, Mister Davenport, would you please smile for the camera?"

"No, no, we hide the camera. We film him."

Budge sat there looking at me. "That's it?"

"What do you mean?"

"That's your plan? Why don't we try to rob a bank while we're at it, or steal the police chief's car, maybe break into city hall?"

"You think my plan won't work?"

He pushed his fingers through his hair. "Jeezul, Hay, I think it's impossible!"

20

"I 'M NOT SO SURE this is a good idea." Budge looked over his shoulder as if someone was about ready to burst into his room. "Merv would kill me if he found out."

"Your father's not going to find out," I said. "Now quit being such a wuss and help me out here."

I was already halfway out the bedroom window, just a few feet above the roof of his father's garden shed. I hung on to the windowsill with my good arm while Budge held on to the sling we had fashioned from a bed sheet and wrapped around my body. "Let me down slowly," I whispered.

It was not easy to make my way down from the second floor of his house with a fractured arm, but Budge carefully let out the line until I was squatting on the roof of the shed. I untied the sheet, caught my breath, and eased myself over the edge of the shed. It was a small shed. Only a short drop. Once I was on the ground, he sent down the backpack. He pulled the sheet in, tied it around the backpack and let it down out the window. I grabbed it and untied it. I looked up at him framed in the window.

"Come on, hurry up," I whispered.

With two good arms he had no trouble climbing out the window. He soon joined me in the backyard. Crickets were chirping all around us, but other than that, it was quiet. A full moon cast our thin shadows across the yard. I'm not sure exactly what time it was, but it could not have been too late since Budge's parents usually went to bed early and they were already asleep. A light still burned in the room shared by Karen and Rachel, so we were extra quiet as we passed beneath it.

Budge's bike stood on the front porch. He put on the backpack and mounted the bicycle. I tried to climb on, too. That was part of the plan, to ride double to the castle. The problem was that my wrist hurt more than I thought it would as I tried to grip the handlebars. More than that, we were simply too big to ride double.

"Darn! This isn't going to work. We're just going to have to walk."

"I don't know why I let you talk me into these things," Budge said. He got off the bike. As we started down the road, he looked back, and I'm sure he thought he would never see his home again. He was that kind of worrier.

There were no streetlights, and if there hadn't been a full moon we might not have been able to see where we were going.

"What if a cop stops us?"

"He won't," I said.

"Why not?"

"He just won't." Apparently, repetition was all the assurance Budge needed since he didn't ask again.

There was little traffic, thankfully. Walking in the dark like this, even with a full moon, wasn't a smart thing to do. We continued in silence for a while. I heard Budge huffing and puffing behind me.

I hadn't forgotten about his heart condition. "Are you alright?"

"Yeah, I'm fine."

He didn't sound fine to me. "I'm sorry I made you walk. You probably could have ridden ahead of me."

"It's okay. The next part is all downhill."

I knew his adrenaline was pumping. Mine too—we were having an adventure. I could already imagine the newspaper headlines: *Local Boys Capture Crooked Mayor.* Maybe we'd get a medal. I could see Ama and the other girls surrounding me, asking a million questions. *Weren't you afraid? Did you fight the mayor? Did he have a gun? Were you hurt?* And there would be Sean Baer, standing off to one side, looking as though his whole world had come to an end.

I could also imagine how proud Mom would be. Oh, sure, I guess I would catch some heat from her for lying and sneaking around, but, considering the result, I'm sure she would think the end justified the means. Dad, too, would be proud.

It seemed like it was taking us forever to get to the castle, but then I saw that we were on Rich Road, turning onto Mulberry. We were practically there. The road was steep and winding, with hairpin turns. I took the backpack from Budge—that was the least I could do—and slipped it on. We carefully picked our way down in the darkness. An owl hooted somewhere nearby and gave us a start.

We reached Shore Road at the bottom of the hill. On our right, the tower of Chateau Laroche stood silhouetted against the moon. Remaining hidden in the dark shadows as much as we could, we cautiously made our way to the castle. We paused in the shelter of the trees just beyond the courtyard.

"Sure is quiet," Budge said, softly. "I don't think anyone is here."

"Maybe, maybe not. Let's get closer and check it out."

"Are you sure, dude?"

My heart was racing, but yes, I was sure.

We crept closer and it became obvious we were alone.

"What now?" Budge said. "We go home?"

"No, of course not. We've got to stay. The mayor has to get the money before the big show tomorrow, right? I mean, that's what I would do if was him, wouldn't you?" He shrugged. "He may have already been here and we missed him," I said. "I hope not. We'd never find the money that way. But if he hasn't been here yet, there's a good chance he will be soon. We need to be ready for him."

I set the backpack on the cobblestones and opened it. "Mom's recorder," I said, holding it up. "Let's put it in the stables again. What do you think?" He didn't answer. "Budge?" I looked up.

He wasn't looking at me, but was gazing toward the stables, a strange look in his eyes. His face seemed paler than usual. *Oh, no, his heart!*

"Budge! Hey, man, are you okay? What is it?"

His words were slow in coming. "I thought I saw something." He kept his eyes trained on the arch leading to the stables.

"What?" I said, looking in the same direction.

"I don't know. I thought I saw a white misty thing. Didn't you see it?"

"No."

"It seemed to glow. I only saw it for a second and then it was gone."

He was creeping me out. "Moonlight?"

He turned back to me, his eyes wide. "Or Sir Harry?"

"So, you don't want to go into the stables?"

He swallowed hard. "That's the place that makes the most sense for the recorder, whether I want to go or not."

I slapped him on the shoulder. "Spoken like a true ghosthunter," I said, trying to give him a shot of bravery despite the fact I was nervous about going in there myself. I would never admit that to him.

There was nothing but darkness beneath the arch leading to the stables. Moonlight could not reach into its depths. In a rush to leave my house, I had forgotten my large flashlight, so we stumbled through the arch, led only by the feeble light from a small penlight I had in my backpack.

"Ouch! Jeezul!" Budge tripped and bumped into me. "Careful where you step, Hay."

I pointed the penlight at the ground and saw some broken stones scattered around. "Were those here last time?"

"I don't remember."

I shined the light on the walls. All I saw was row after row of stone, and one large spider that skittered out of the light. Nothing looked suspicious, or out of place, but it was hard to tell for sure in such weak light.

"You getting anything?" I asked, seeing that Budge seemed to be more sensitive than I was to anything, or anyone, that might be there. He cocked his head to one side, listening for something, and then shook his head *no*, his shadow on the wall imitating the gesture.

"Alright, how about up there?" I pointed to a wooden support beam that angled up from the wall to the roof. "Give me a boost."

I turned the recorder on as he locked his hands together. I braced my foot in his hands. With a grunt, he hoisted me up and I quickly placed the recorder in the crook of the beam. "Sorry, man, I know this is hard for you," I said, after Budge let me down.

"Let's get out of here."

A high wall across the courtyard marked the castle's boundary. It ran parallel to Shore Road, which ended in a turn-around in front of the castle. A small square tower set with a gate was built into the center of the wall, with several steps leading up from the road to the courtyard. Entering through the gate, you could go straight ahead into the courtyard, or you could continue up to the top of the tower where you had a clear view of the road on one side and the castle grounds on the other. That's where we decided to set up our observation post.

We sat in the corner, trying to keep ourselves hidden in shadow, and talked quietly while we waited.

"What do we do if the mayor shows up?" Budge asked.

"We don't do anything but get him on video. Then we give it to Mom. She'll take it from there."

"Do you think he'll go to jail?"

"He took money from Mister Ambrose. That's a bribe, and taking a bribe is illegal. He'll go to jail."

"I hope so, because Merv will really be p.o.'d if he finds out about this and we don't get anything out of it."

I knew how he felt. "Yeah, Mom will be, too. But what are we supposed to do, just let it happen and not do anything?"

He didn't answer. I wondered if maybe he thought that, yes, that would be a good idea. We should mind our own business. How was the mayor's taking a bribe hurting us, anyway? Was Budge right? It made me mad to think that a guy like Mayor Davenport, a smarmy kind of guy who was downright mean to Mom and the other women on city council, should get away with something like that. He was a crook. Shouldn't we try to stop crooks?

I believed Dad would try to stop the mayor. He might go about it in a different way, since he was a grown-up, but I was sure he wouldn't let it go. Dad might wear glasses and be a quiet kind of guy, but I knew that inside he's a fighter. Many times, I've heard him giving support and advice to Mom as she worked on some of the city's problems. He would absolutely fight the mayor on this bribery thing, and if *he* would, then I should, too. Dad was off in Afghanistan being a different kind of fighter. He couldn't do anything about the mayor, but I could.

"Don't worry, Budge. We're doing the right thing."

We hunkered down in the shadows. It was a cool night, and a breeze came up off the river now and then, giving me goosebumps. The camcorder lay at my feet, ready to go when we needed it. We sat there quietly, trying to stay awake as the night wore on. I heard the river gurgling over stones, the crickets singing in the grass, and the spooky hooting of that owl again. And then, we heard car tires crunching on gravel.

21

"**D**UCK, BUDGE!"

We crouched behind the parapet, peeking through its notches to the tree-shadowed road below. A car drove slowly through the turnaround and then came to a stop before the castle. I grabbed the camcorder and cautiously aimed it through a notch. The car's engine turned off and the lights went out. Moonlight glinted on the car's trim, but it was still too dark for me to tell its color. The car may have been a Lexus—just like the mayor's—but I couldn't be sure.

"Is it the mayor?" Budge whispered.

We heard the car door open. I zoomed in with the camera. Squinty eyes, bristly little moustache. It was the mayor, alright. In the camera's viewfinder, we seemed to be almost face to face, and when he glanced up toward the wall, I felt sure that he was looking right into my eyes. My heart skidded inside my chest. I was about ready to jump up and tell Budge to run like hell, but then the mayor looked away and I realized he hadn't seen us. At least not yet.

"What's he doing now?"

"He's just standing there, looking around," I whispered. "Uh-oh, here he comes. Don't move!"

I slid down beside him, the two of us holding our breath, afraid to move a muscle. On the other side of the wall, we heard the mayor's footsteps on gravel, then the clanking of the metal chain that secured the front gate directly below as he fiddled with it. My heart pounded like it would explode. I felt faint from holding my breath. The mayor swore softly and then the clanking stopped. His footsteps faded away.

"He's probably going to go around the wall through the driveway entrance," I said. "Maybe we can get him on camera as he comes into the courtyard." I scooted over to the wall facing the driveway and parking lot. A locked gate—only an iron bar—kept cars out, but a person could easily climb over the bar and get onto the castle grounds.

Sure enough, there was Mayor Davenport creeping up from the driveway. I aimed the camcorder at him and let it roll. Even when I zoomed in on him, he was still far away. He was wearing dark clothes, too, but at least I was using a night vision setting—just like the ghosthunters did—so I was certain we would record something.

Budge was on all fours beside me now, looking out over the parapet. "He's heading for the stables." He sat cross-legged behind the parapet, leaning toward me so that his head wouldn't show above the wall. "What do we do now?"

I knelt behind the wall, keeping the camera trained on the mayor, who was carefully making his way across the courtyard toward the archway into the stables. Every few steps, he would stop and turn around, as though he thought he was being followed.

"I guess we should follow him."

"Oh, Jeezul, Hay, do you really think so?" The fear in his voice made me nervous. "What if he sees us? What if he has a gun?"

"Mayor Davenport with a gun? Don't be ridiculous."

"Did you ever think the mayor would be a criminal?"

"No, probably not."

"Did you ever think your father would be roaming around in Afghanistan toting a gun?"

"No."

"Then why do you think it's so unlikely that the mayor might have a gun? This is America, dude; *everyone* has a gun."

I guess he had a point. I had been a Boy Scout for a short time, and I recalled their motto: *Be prepared.* It seemed lame at the time. Be prepared for what? But now I saw that it meant being prepared for *anything,* including the unlikely possibility that a loser like Mayor Davenport might be carrying a gun.

I sighed and sat beside him. "Alright, do you have a better idea?" I glanced back and saw that the mayor was now lost in the shadow of the castle.

He took his cell phone out of his pocket. "We call the police."

"And tell them what? *Uh, hello? Police department? Yeah, I'm calling to tell you that the mayor is at the Loveland Castle taking bribe money out of the walls.* What do you think they would say to a call like that?"

"I don't know. They'd check it out, wouldn't they?"

"Oh sure, and when they ask you your name and age and you tell them that you're twelve years old, they'll come running, of course. They wouldn't think for one minute that we were pranking them, would they?"

"Would they think that?" he asked, my sarcasm bouncing off his thick skull.

"Forget it, Budge. We can't call the police. They'd never buy it."

I looked over the wall and could no longer see the mayor. I didn't know if he was still in the courtyard or if he had entered the stables. I would have to get closer to find out where he'd gone.

"Look, Budge, we need to get the mayor on camera retrieving the money. Showing him walking around the castle in the middle of the night might make an interesting, even weird video, but it doesn't prove anything. It certainly doesn't prove that he's a criminal. We need hard evidence."

He wasn't happy. He looked down at his feet. "Fine," he said, quietly.

"I'm going to follow him." Even as I said those words, my knees felt weak.

"I was afraid you were going to say that."

"You don't have to come with me. You've got the cell phone. You can wait right here while I follow him. I'll stay out of sight, but if I need help, then call the police. I'll yell or something."

"That's it? That's your plan? You'll yell or something?"

I nodded.

"Merv will kill us both," Budge said.

"Okay, here goes." I grabbed the camera and slowly rose to my feet. I was just going to take the first step down from the tower when I froze.

Headlights were coming down Shore Road toward the castle.

I stood there unable to move, watching the lights draw closer. I wondered who it could be—Mister Ambrose? It didn't make sense that he would be here again, but if not him, then who? The vehicle passed below the castle wall, drove through the turnaround and came to a stop in front of the mayor's car. Even before I saw the soccer ball decal in the back window, I recognized Mom's SUV.

I felt cold inside, as though everything had turned to stone.

"Who is it?" Budge whispered.

"Mom!"

"What?" Forgetting himself, he sprang to his feet and looked over the parapet. "What's *she* doing here? Did you tell her what we were doing?"

I grabbed his shirt and yanked him back down. "No, of course not."

But what *was* Mom doing here? We watched as she got out of the van. I wanted to call out to her, but the words caught in my throat. I didn't know what to say. She was wearing jeans and a dark top, as though wanting to blend into the shadows. A small purse hung from her shoulder. She stood by the door for a moment before walking back to the mayor's car.

What the heck is she doing?

Mom approached the mayor's car cautiously, like she was walking by a sleeping pit bull. She looked through the car windows, then turned toward the castle. If she had looked up, she might have seen me and Budge gawking like idiots, but she seemed focused on something else. She must have noticed the locked gate because she started slowly walking down the road toward the castle driveway, following the same path the mayor had taken.

"What's she doing?" Budge said.

"I wish I knew," I said, softly.

"Haycorn … what if your mother …" His voice trailed off.

I turned to him. "What if my mother what?" I said, looking straight into his eyes.

He glanced away. "Nothing."

I stepped closer to him. "No, Budge, tell me what you were going to say. What about my mother?"

"Jeezul, Haycorn, I don't know." He took a step back. "What if she's part of it?"

Had anyone else said those words to me, I would have thrown them off the tower. As it was, I had pushed him to say them, and I knew why. It was because that same awful suspicion had taken hold of me, too, but I couldn't bring myself to admit it. It sure seemed suspicious Mom would come to the castle just when the mayor was retrieving the money. With Dad in Afghanistan and not working, I knew things were a little tight for us money-wise. She worried about that. Maybe she had figured out a way to get some of Mister Ambrose's money.

"Haycorn?"

I ignored him. Maybe Mom used the recording to scare the mayor into giving her some of the money. She could have threatened to give the recording to the police if he didn't give her any. I couldn't imagine for one minute that she would have done such a thing, but as Budge had pointed out, a lot had come to pass that I could not have imagined, either. *Be prepared.*

"I'm sorry, Haycorn, but you asked."

"Shut up."

Mom had said I shouldn't get involved in this whole mess. It was a problem for adults to solve, for her to solve. Thinking about what she had said, I wondered now what she meant when she said she would handle it. I thought she meant she would make sure the mayor got caught, but maybe that's not at all what she meant. Maybe that's why she wanted me and Budge to stay out of it, because she was just as much a crook as Mayor Davenport.

My body felt like it weighed a ton. I was filled with sadness. I slunk down against the parapet and sat on the floor. My eyes filled with tears. I didn't want to cry, I really didn't, but the tears came anyway, and I sat there like a baby, sobbing quietly. What was I supposed to do now? I wished with all my heart Dad was there.

Budge squatted down beside me. "Listen, Hay, I didn't mean what I said." I couldn't answer. "It was just a crazy thought."

I barely heard his words at the edge of my black thoughts.

He put his hand on my shoulder. "Come on, man, this is your mother we're talking about. You know her, you know how she is. Do you really think she's involved with a weasel like Mayor Davenport?"

"I don't know," I said, sniffling.

"Yes, you do." He squeezed my shoulder.

I looked up at him. In the moonlight, his blue eyes seemed to glow. I wiped my good hand across my eyes. "But what's she doing here, then?"

He shrugged and smiled. "What are *we* doing here?"

I sat there for a few moments, looking across the shadowed courtyard toward the stables. I didn't see the mayor or Mom. What if she was there to catch the mayor, after all? Maybe I was wrong to doubt her.

Just then we heard a scraping sound, metal on stone, coming to us from across the courtyard. We looked at each other.

"The mayor. It must be. He's digging in the wall!"

I got to my feet. The sound echoed again in the courtyard, and, at the same time, I saw movement in the shadows by the driveway.

Mom was sneaking across the courtyard.

22

NO TIME NOW. Mom was approaching the arch leading to the stables. If she was truly trying to catch the mayor in the act, she was being foolish about it. How did she think she would stop him? Whack him with her purse? She was in trouble.

"I've got to go to her, Budge!"

He nodded. "Right. I've got the cell phone."

In the back of my mind there was still that small doubt about why she was at the castle, so I wasn't sure I wanted the police to come barging in on her. "Okay, but don't use it right away. You remember my signal?'

"Yeah, you'll yell or something."

Good enough for Budge. "Yes."

"Be careful," he said, as I crept down the tower steps.

I carried the camcorder and paused to take a shot of Mom inching her way closer to the arch. I watched on the screen until I saw her disappear in the darkness. The moon had traveled across the sky, casting longer shadows over the courtyard, so I was able to make my way to the stable in almost complete darkness. I heard scraping sounds again from inside the castle.

I hadn't noticed it before but as I drew closer to the arch, I saw a glow coming from within. A flashlight, or maybe a lantern of some kind. The light wasn't bright but probably enough to allow the mayor to dig out the money. I heard footsteps somewhere ahead of me. *Mom*, I thought. I couldn't rush in to confront her and the mayor until I was absolutely certain of her motives. So, just inside the arch, I stopped to listen.

More scraping, and then the scratching sound of something being dragged over stone. Suddenly, a flash of light exploded in the gloomy interior of the stables—a camera flash, I was certain— and for a moment, I saw the silhouettes of two people.

The mayor swore. I heard something heavy drop to the ground.

"Smile," I heard Mom say.

Everything went quiet for a moment. In the stillness my ears strained to hear something. When Mayor Davenport responded, his voice was cool and calm.

"Well, look who's here. If it isn't Councilwoman Smith."

I didn't like the tone of his voice. I edged closer and noticed in the middle of a subtler glow a small lantern on the ground. Two pairs of legs shifted in its dim light.

"I got you, Lee," Mom said. "I've got you here on camera."

"So I see." I heard him moving around in the shadows. "What exactly do you think you have, Mrs. Smith?"

I couldn't tell what he was doing, or what *she* was doing for that matter, but the way the mayor spoke to her made me think he was not afraid. Not the least bit rattled.

"I know all about the bribe you took from Ambrose," Mom said.

Keeping my back pressed to the wall, I crept closer, still hidden in shadow. I could see them better now, two figures less than four feet apart. The light from the lantern reflected off a metal briefcase lying at the mayor's feet. A small pickaxe leaned against the wall. The figures wavered, but I couldn't tell if they were moving or if it was an effect of the light.

"That briefcase is full of money, isn't it?" she said.

To my surprise, the mayor calmly replied, "Why, yes, it is, one hundred thousand dollars to be exact."

"I knew it!" Mom said, more to herself than to the mayor.

"You knew it. And now … what?"

I stood there listening, and finally remembered I was still carrying the camcorder. I turned it on.

"And now we go to the police." She sounded as though she had the situation under control, so I remained hidden from view.

The mayor laughed. It's never a good sign when the bad guy laughs.

"Really?"

I could imagine the smirk on his face, even though I couldn't see it.

He bent down and picked up the case. Mom stepped back. He held it in front of him and opened it. "Take a good look, Anne. One hundred … thousand … dollars."

I saw her take a step closer. She lifted one hand and there was the flash again as she took a picture of the money. I flattened myself against the wall when the flash went off, afraid to breathe. They didn't see me.

"Cute," said the mayor. "Have you ever seen so much money at one time? There's so much here that if, let's say, ten thousand dollars, went missing, why I wouldn't even notice it, if you catch my drift."

She laughed. Why? Did she think that wasn't enough?

The mayor chuckled. "You're a player, Mrs. Smith. I wouldn't have thought that. Good for you. How about twenty thousand?"

He was trying to buy her silence. That proved she wasn't part of the bribery scheme! She *was* at the castle trying to catch him red-handed. And she had! All my doubts lifted at once. I was about to stand up and reveal myself, shout out a war whoop or something, when an odd sensation enveloped me. It felt as though the air around me had grown thick, as though I were buried in Jell-O. At the same time, the temperature in the stables suddenly dropped—and I mean *a lot*! It was so cold my breath came out in frosty little clouds.

Mom and the mayor felt it too. I heard him mutter, "What the …?" Then, remembering what he was doing here, he said to Mom, "Twenty thousand dollars. It's yours. Go on. *Take it!*" He pushed the case toward her. "All you have to do is reach in, take the money, and walk out of here. Keep your mouth shut. It's all very simple."

I was still confused by how the atmosphere in the room had changed. A breeze off the river? And the room seemed to be filling with fog. I crept a few inches along the wall and started when I bumped into someone. "Budge!" I hissed, under my breath.

"Sorry, Hay," he whispered.

Mom said, "I've called the police, Lee. They're on their way."

The mayor nonchalantly shut the case and set it down on the ground. He lifted the pickaxe. "No, they're not. You didn't call them. But you should have." He lunged at her.

I couldn't tell what happened next. Just as I broke from the shadows, yelling, *Mom! Run!* with Budge practically on my back, the fog swirled into something like the shape of a man in the space between the mayor and Mom. It hovered there, startling the mayor just as he was about to swing the pickaxe. In that moment all three of us darted through the arch. In the commotion I dropped the camera.

"Go! Go!" I shouted, pushing Budge forward. Mom was already a few steps ahead of us.

I saw the sleeve of her sweater was torn. I looked over my shoulder and saw the mayor charging out of the stables, the pickaxe in his hand. Behind him, a luminous shape seemed to pounce on his back. He stumbled over something on the floor and went down with a grunt.

Okay, I know it was a dumb thing to do, but when I saw him go down and thought of him trying to kill my mother, I totally lost it. Rushing over to him—yelling something, I don't know what—I yanked the pickaxe from his hand and heaved it into the darkness. It clanged somewhere far off. For good measure, with the mayor on all fours glaring at me, I kicked him in the knee as hard as I could. Then ran like hell.

Mom turned to see where I was, but I yelled for her to keep running, *get to the car!* Budge was panting along beside me. I glanced back again and saw the mayor stagger to his feet. At the same time, red and blue flashing lights strobed through the trees above the castle. *The cops!* The mayor hobbled around in the courtyard, looking for his lost weapon. If he was aware of the police descending on the castle, he paid them no mind. The dude was possessed.

The three of us kept running. We made it to the driveway, panting breathlessly, just as the first patrol car raced down Shore Road, lights flashing. Three more cars arrived and blocked the road while the officers spilled out, running onto the castle grounds. One of them stopped to check on us. We were just standing in the driveway now, catching our breath. I realized I'd never seen Mom run so fast in my life.

I looked back into the courtyard and saw the officers' searchlights crisscrossing the grounds. There was no sign of the mayor. *Oh, Jeezul, he got away!* Then I saw the lights bobbing among the garden terraces and heard the radio worn by the officer standing next to us crackle. *We got him.*

Mom hugged me, Budge too. It felt good— until her mood suddenly turned. "And what were you two doing here?" Her eyes bored into mine. "Didn't I tell you to leave it alone? Didn't I?"

"Yes," I said, quietly.

"Haycorn, you could have been hurt ... or worse." She was angry, so angry there were tears in her eyes.

"We just wanted to help," I said, but I was crying too. I was only just starting to realize the danger we'd all been in. I didn't feel much like a hero at all.

Budge stood there, not speaking, pale as a ghost. He was probably imagining what Merv would say when he found out what we'd been up to.

"I know you did," Mom said, softening just a bit, "but what you did was stupid. Worse, you disobeyed me, and that really hurts."

I didn't know what to say. She was right, of course, but hadn't Budge and I just helped prevent something a lot worse?

The officers were coming back across the courtyard, two of them walking Mayor Davenport between them, arms handcuffed behind his back. He gave Mom a cold look as he passed by but didn't say anything.

She watched as the officers assisted him into the back seat of a patrol car then turned to us and sighed. "Well, at least you're safe."

When she smiled, weakly, I hugged her. She was still angry, I knew, Snake-Eyes and all, and she might be angry with me for quite a while. I would probably have to earn her trust all over again. Still, I knew we would make it in the long run. I pulled away far enough to smile back.

"It's a good thing you called the police, Mom."

"Me? I didn't call them. I thought you did."

"No ..."

"*I* called them," Budge said.

I turned to him. "But I didn't give you the signal."

He looked away then right into my eyes. "I know, but when I saw your mom there and you went after her, I guess I just got scared. I called the cops almost as soon as you left."

"It's a good thing you did," Mom said.

"Mrs. Smith? Could I have a word with you?" said one of the officers.

"Of course." Mom walked off to the officer's patrol car.

Budge and I stood there in the driveway, looking up at the castle. The other police cars were already driving away. Once again, the night was settling down quietly around the castle.

"And the cops believed you?" I said to Budge. "Amazing."

"They believed *Mister* Shifflet," he said, lowering his voice to a dead-on impersonation of his father.

"Nice going, dude."

"So, are we going to talk about the other thing?"

"What other thing?" I said, but I wasn't looking at him. Instead, I focused on the white blur of an owl gliding from the trees above the castle.

"You know. Sir Harry."

I didn't answer right away. The owl disappeared. "You saw it, too?" I said finally.

"Yes. Harry saved our lives."

A ghost saved our lives. How could we ever explain that to anyone who hadn't seen it with their own eyes? How could I explain it to our friends? To Ama? To Dad? Everyone would think I was crazy. We were both crazy.

"Nobody will believe us, you know."

Budge shrugged and looked up at the sky. "No, probably not."

"Wait a minute. The camcorder! I dropped it back there!"

We ran back across the courtyard and found the camera lying by the arch. I grabbed it and turned it on. Tried to turn it on. "What the ...?"

"Bad news, man," Budge said. "See that little red light? That means the battery is dead."

"The light was red when I had the camera inside ... Oh, no! I thought that meant the camera was *on*."

"Nope. Ancient Chinese proverb: a red light is never a good sign."

I sighed. "At least the recorder we set up will prove the Mayor was guilty. We just can't prove that a ghost saved our lives."

153

Budge put his hand on my shoulder. "No, we can't. But we know."

Mom called us. The remaining patrol car backed down out of the driveway. I took one last look at the castle, the tower outlined against the sky that was now turning pearly gray, the arch to the stables dark again.

Good-bye, Harry, and thank you.

AUTHOR'S NOTE

Although Loveland, Ohio and Chateau Laroche are real places, this novel is a work of fiction. All the characters in this book, except Harry Andrews, are fictitious, products of the author's imagination. Any resemblance to any person living or dead is unintentional and purely coincidental.

Chateau Laroche, originally built by Harry Andrews, still stands in Loveland, and is today maintained by the Knights of the Golden Trail. I once lived in Loveland, visited the castle several times, and met Sir Harry, as well as some of the Knights. Although I do poke fun of the Knights, I have only the deepest respect and admiration for the work they have done in keeping Sir Harry's dream alive. I encourage you to visit Chateau Laroche if you are ever in the greater Cincinnati area.

For more about the hauntings at Chateau Laroche, read *Ghosthunting Ohio: On the Road Again* (Clerisy Press, 2011).

ABOUT THE AUTHOR

John Kachuba is the award-winning author of twelve books of fiction and non-fiction. His most recent work, *Shapeshifters: A History*, was a finalist in the Horror Writers Association's Bram Stoker Award. John holds M.A. degrees in Creative Writing from Antioch University Midwest and Ohio University. He is a frequent speaker at conferences, universities, and libraries, and on podcasts, radio, and television. You can find out more about John on his website, *johnkachuba.com*.

FOR DISCUSSION

1. Haycorn is jealous when he mistakenly thinks that Ama and Sean are girlfriend and boyfriend. Angry, he repeats a harmful rumor about her to Ama and she slaps him. How could each of them have handled their anger better?

2. When Haycorn's father is deployed to Afghanistan, Haycorn feels he must step up to be more helpful to his mother. Do you think he was successful? Why, or why not?

3. Haycorn and Budge are amateur ghosthunters and discover the ghost of Sir Harry at the castle. What would you do if you encountered a ghost?

4. The boys disobey their parents when they sneak out of Budge's house in the middle of the night and go to the castle, trying to find evidence against Mayor Davenport. Even though their intentions were good, were the boys justified in disobeying their parents?

5. After Haycorn's disastrous conversation with Ama at the nature preserve, he is angry with himself for his behavior and feels ashamed. He writes an apologetic letter to Ama. Have you ever been in a situation that made you feel that way? What did you do?

6. What do you think makes Haycorn and Budge such good friends?

YOU MIGHT ALSO ENJOY

THE SMUGGLERS
FROM THE "TRUCK STOP AT THE CENTER OF THE GALAXY"

by Vanessa MacLaren-Wray

Attachment is everything.

Mother says, "Don't name the merchandise," and "Don't let the humans see you."

Available from Water Dragon Publishing in
hardcover, trade paperback, and digital editions
waterdragonpublishing.com

Printed in the USA
CPSIA information can be obtained
at www.ICGtesting.com
JSHW021050091123
51467JS00001B/33